Praise for *Po*

"A mouthwatering tale with flavo ... ...u *Under the Tuscan Sun* . . . sinfully sweet and satisfying." —*Orlando Sentinel*

"Glorious, daring, and delightful, filled with humor, hope, and possibility." —Adriana Trigiani, author of the Big Stone Gap novels

"An enchanting tale of love, family, and renewal." —Firoozeh Dumas, author of *Laughing Without an Accent*

"Beautiful strangers bring exotic recipes to town in Mehran's foodie-lit debut . . . fans of *Chocolat* and other cooking-overcomes-cultural-differences stories will savor the tale." —*Publishers Weekly*

Praise for *Rosewater and Soda Bread*

"Mehran's novel delights the senses on every page. The story pulses with life as three Iranian sisters struggle to make sense of matters of the heart and the spirit." —Elizabeth Cox, author of *The Slow Moon*

"I would recommend this book for gourmands, anyone interested in Irish culture, those who are fascinated by what happens when cultures from thousands of miles apart meet—and by how sharing a meal can help break down even the most seemingly insurmountable barriers." —*Blogging for a Good Book*

The Saturday Night School of Beauty

ALSO BY MARSHA MEHRAN

Pomegranate Soup

Rosewater and Soda Bread

The Saturday Night School of Beauty

MARSHA MEHRAN

with an Afterword by Abbas Mehran

amazon crossing

Previously published as *The Margaret Thatcher School of Beauty* by Harper Collins in Australia in 2014.

"Another Birth" by Forugh Farrokhzad, first published in Persian in 1964; English translation from Michael Craig Hillmann's *A Lonely Woman: Forugh Farrokhzad and Her Poetry* (1987).

Published by AmazonCrossing, Seattle

www.apub.com

Amazon, the Amazon logo, and AmazonCrossing are trademarks of Amazon.com, Inc., or its affiliates.

ISBN-13: 9781503947146
ISBN-10: 1503947149

Cover design by David Drummond

Printed in the United States of America

Chapter One

The pulling of the thread was one of the first lessons Zadi Heirati learned in the *hammam*, the bathhouse. She had been working at the hammam for only a month when she came to learn the meaning of the *band*, the thread, the soliloquy of its art, the art of removing body hair, called *band andazi*.

Zadi had come to the hammam from Hamedan, the city where she was born. She took a bus to the capital, arriving at its concave and congested central station, with its blooming arches and strange memorials, and took a city bus to one of the northern suburbs called Tajrish, where she had heard there were wealthier residents. The choice of the wealthier area of the capital was not instinctual, for she would have rather headed south, where flowers sprouted from the corners of brick buildings, like perennials of Roman statues, and stray children ran and played in the streets, screaming obscenities peppered with poetic knowledge. No, the choice of the north came from a need to alter her own internal compass, as she had decided she no longer trusted its strangely vacillating and often derogatory commands. In turning north, pushing against the tide, she felt that twist within her very being.

The bus Zadi had taken from Hamedan had traveled over the rambling Alvand Mountains, snowy and precipitous terrain littered with primeval villages, had been erected during the time of the ancients and had for the most part been left unchanged. The passing stones and vegetation reminded Zadi of an afternoon a few days prior, when she had been sitting on the back porch of a house she had known for a while. It was a place of particular quiescence. She was sitting on the back porch with a bowl of broad beans. She had pushed the beans out of their skins in preparation for the springtime feast. Accidentally, she had spilled the beans onto the terracotta tiles and had stood up in fright and disbelief. In her mind now, on the bus, she could see the pods growing stalks in the harsh cold, shooting up between the tiles into the spring air, and the tragic scene unfolding around them. She had stood up in awe and trepidation. But as she sat in that hurtling bus heading toward the capital, she wondered. The beginning is the ending, the poet had said. She had always known, thought Zadi, that from the moment she arrived at her grandmother's house, she was on her way out of it.

It is what it is.

What it was, was eternal banishment—and there is nothing wrong with eternal banishment.

After alighting at the last bus station in Tajrish, Zadi made her way on foot through the town, which teemed with the day's festivities, and turned north, not because she knew where she was going, but because it was the direction that suddenly brought her back a deep feeling from inside. At the end of a long, narrow street—Poplar Street, flanked by poplars heavy with ripening flowers—she saw the small dome, its bell shape rusted by rain, the patina dulled and beautiful. Her mind was on what was behind her, so she did not realize that she was standing before the hammam's door until it opened. Zadi, who had until that morning thought proverbs to be mere ornaments to everyday life, was taken aback when a woman opened the door and spoke.

"I used to feel sorry for myself because I had no shoes," the woman said.

"Until I met a man who was dead," Zadi replied, understanding as she did that the words uttered were the very reason for their being.

Yes, it was a hammam. There was a position available, for a strong girl. "Step forward," the woman said. "And don't mind the *jennies* lurking in the shadows."

Mina Nazeri, forty-nine, had been working at the hammam for thirty years and had learned all the secrets of her profession. She was a vivacious, strong matriarch of resilience, courage, and determination and had earned the obedience and respect of her employees and clients. Everyone called her *Khanoum*, a reverential title for women of high quality. Khanoum Mina not only had a thorough knowledge of the secrets of beauty, of recipes, ingredients, and treatments; but she also knew the history of the hammam.

When the Arab Caliph Umar invaded the Sassanian Empire in the seventh century, the hammam had already been operating its healing fonts for a hundred years, pulling from the hot springs on which it was built the essence of waters and oils that dispensed the kind of healing capabilities only known among the priesthood of a certain celestial being.

As the forces of turbaned men stormed the Zagros Mountains and the rest of the vast Iranian plateau, the women who oversaw the bathhouse shut the cedar doors and barred them with boulders, so as to keep the army away from their usual medicine of pillage and rape.

The hammam's doors did not keep out the caliphate's army; the two dozen women in the hammam were raped and hung from the boughs of the poplars surrounding the stony fountains and returning terraces.

But the waters—their enticement persisted. Many of the caliph's men were tempted to jump into the pools of steaming mineral-rich liquid, wrapping themselves in the refined ways of the locals, donning themselves in nuances of faith and etiquette. These men, and the rest of the horde that hurried its way from the south, did not know that what they were gaining was something quite mysterious, something that was not easily measured but could perhaps be found over and around those very healing waters.

It is the nearness that I treasure.

Once the caliph's army was gone, and the poplars held only a song of their terrible leaves, a woman by the name of Anahita the Great took it upon herself to open those cedar doors again.

The hammam on Poplar Street was one of the finest in Tehran. It consisted of five acres of prime northern land, half of which was taken up by a maze of buildings, with rooms opening into each other at every turn.

Having established herself in the small nook given to her as a sleeping quarter, across the courtyard from the main hammam building, Zadi began the lengthy process of learning about the hammam's myriad traditions. Among them was band andazi, one of the most popular with the clientele of neighborhood housewives and virgins.

Band andazi, or threading, begins with a preparation of rosewater and powder. A rice pudding of a paste, this mixture has been known to provoke grumbles of hunger in many a confused stomach. Once treated with a coating of the mixture, the thread is then ready for assembling.

The day Zadi truly began to understand the band had begun just as always in the hammam, with Zadi completing the last stages of this preparation for her client, a corpulent matron who favored long massage treatments and who was a virgin to the thread. Its opening and closing web proved far too drastic, too barbaric, for her refined tastes. Taking one look at the scissorlike string coming her way, she fainted. Not an uncommon reaction to band andazi; one in every three of the hammam's clients succumbed to their flight instinct.

Zadi was practiced in the arena of reviving; she gently rolled the frightened woman onto her side, onto a cushioned divan, especially made for just this purpose, that ran along the perimeters of the room. Uncorking a tiny glass flask of *atr*, the essence of Caspian roses, she held the perfume to the somnolescent nostrils, allowing the magic of the exalted petals, which had been treated to the salted breezes of the Caspian Sea, to reach into the mind's sleeping recesses. Only seconds were needed for the woman to awake, to overcome her timidity and nod *yes*. Of course not every client fainted. Plenty of bathers were all too willing to submit themselves to bracing tugs of the twisting thread. Despite their show of courage, Zadi knew the real reason why some of her clients were so willing: there are those among us who enjoy pain, who revel in its transitory power to relieve a much deeper malaise. In Zadi's experience, more often than not, these clients were of a defined breed, the wives and daughters of many of Tehran's most prominent men, its crème de la crème.

Having wakened her fainted client in this instance, Zadi found herself considering the ingenuity of band andazi. When all was said and done, it was a simple method: pulling the thread and plucking the hair, a dance that needed the participation of both partners. Often the client would retreat, pulling back as the thread came toward her face. Soon, however, she would inch forward, allowing the threader to move back and forth with her until the face became rosy, engorged, and free of unwanted hair. And it was this dance, Zadi realized, that was the best part of band andazi, for it involved a combined determination. Such a simple notion, yet integral to the completion of the dance.

. . .

As with all, it did not take long for Khanoum Mina to discover the reason Zadi had traveled from Hamedan to work in the hammam. She gave Zadi a stack of books, instructional mostly, on the art of beauty, and directed her to take them back to her small room across the courtyard. The precious texts unfortunately did not do much to help Zadi; try as she might, she could not keep her eyes on the pages before her.

"Do you know why the hammam was built?" Khanoum Mina asked one day as they stood before the threshold of the hot room.

"To cleanse the body and the spirit that follows," said Zadi, staring at the amalgam of mosaics spreading out in infinite directions above her head.

"That is what we tell them—what we let them think. But that is not the truth." Khanoum Mina smiled. "It's about the particles, the ones we haven't gotten a hold of yet. And never will."

Zadi did not understand what particles Khanoum Mina was talking about. She had knowledge of hammam, of course; suspended in the corner of her mind was the sweet and distant memory of one afternoon with her mother, who had taken her to the mountain springs of her hometown, in which there were several mineral baths similar to the ones in Tehran. But nothing in that remembrance had involved the kind of mysterious phenomena Khanoum Mina was referring to.

It was not until a few days later that Zadi came to understand Khanoum Mina's words.

That was the day Khanoum Mina summoned her to the bridal quarter. After receiving many treatments, the bridal party had gathered at the center of the hammam. It was customary for the party to partake of all the hammam's services before having the henna. The party had lasted the whole morning and afternoon, and Zadi felt tired. A chill permeated her insides. She felt the wrenching in her stomach again, a hollow that had been present for months. The coldness running throughout her body seemed to have worsened during the course of the day, leaving her freezing as she stood there in the cooling room. Her long, tentlike dress covered her burgeoning belly. As the sun set through the ironwork windows that lined the upper tiers of the domed ceiling, Zadi turned a corner into the inner bridal quarter. What she saw there made her knees weaken and tremble.

The young bride's jubilant and rosy-cheeked face was being laid down on a soft mattress by her female relatives. The treatment was hard and soft at the same time, like a marriage, Khanoum Mina was saying. In a distant corner a woman hired especially for the occasion thumped on a *tombak* drum, a beat that had its genesis in an understanding of desire. As the drumbeats deepened in both tempo and rhythm, the bride's gown was opened to reveal her body ready for the henna brush.

One by one her female relatives took turns, dipping the brush into the plates of red paste. Blood red, for the blood of the generations, Khanoum Mina had told Zadi. "The pure love that carries through all time."

An utter sadness filled Zadi then, meeting the coldness somewhere in her middle, where the baby who was growing inside of her, perhaps aware of the dichotomy, kicked violently.

Pure love, Khanoum Mina had said. Zadi could hardly believe she had ever been cared for with such deference, let alone remember what it felt like. That's what happens when your heart is broken, she reflected. Your heart lost its beat and its ability to release that enchanting sensation.

And that was when the meaning of Khanoum Mina's words showed itself. The tombak drum was beating its clandestine beat. Taking the brush, the bride's mother touched the young woman's stomach. In that instant, with the dipping of the boiled henna leaves, the connection of the mother's heart to her daughter, love began to flow again. So Khanoum Mina had told Zadi, but it wasn't until that moment, as she watched the henna brush on the young bride, that she understood its power.

As the beams of the sunset filtered through that domed ceiling and the room of women began to sway like a giant sea, the blood within Zadi's own body began to compound. In an instant, warmth overtook her every pore, filling up the cave in her stomach as though it had never been there. Turning on her heels, she ran from the room of women, scurrying into a nearby locker room. There she tore open her work clothes and stared at her stomach.

There, at the precipice that was her pregnant belly, was a trickling, a teardrop colored dark red. Without thinking, she ran back to the bridal party, standing in the doorway while the bride, now fully sanctified, was hugged and kissed by her relatives.

And Zadi knew she had also been blessed, for in that moment, she had seen why she had been placed in the hammam—to learn, to experiment, to acquire experience, and to give back what she had been given. She had seen her purpose.

Giving birth to her daughter, Maryam, was one of the best experiences Zadi could have had. And what a wonderful place to give birth and to be born: in a pool of warm, clean, mineral-rich water, while being blessed by half a dozen naked women.

Khanoum Mina was alert, waiting for any sign of Zadi's impending labor. She knew the difference between false and real contractions. Although she had never been able to give birth herself, she loved to be a midwife, an assistant, or at least an observer. And so she had learned at a much younger age, and had delivered babies before.

As the due date approached, Zadi felt easy contractions. She thought they were real ones and started shouting, but Khanoum Mina tried to calm her, assuring her that the real contractions would be coming soon.

"They are very painful," Khanoum Mina said, shaking her head to emphasize what she meant.

"More pain than this? Oh my God!"

Khanoum Mina had prepared for the delivery, and when the time came—after several strong, painful, and repetitive contractions, minutes apart, during which Zadi could not move—she called the other women to get ready.

"Now is the time. Bring her here!"

The women helped Zadi into a small pool with a fountain of running water. The delivery took half an hour, during which the women called on the divines to ease the pain of Zadi's labor.

Since ancient times, it had been a tradition in Iran to call the divines for help at the time of giving birth. Zoroastrians used to call on the prophet Peer-e Sabz, who was replaced by Hazrat Khezr and, after the invasion of Islam, by Imam Ali.

When Maryam was born, all the women started chanting, crying over and over, "*kli li li li li li li li li*," the chant for happy moments—births and weddings.

The baby was wrapped in a white cloth, and Khanoum Mina was about to bind her body with a rope, when Zadi stopped her. "I don't want my baby to be wrapped in *ghondagh*. I want her to be free, free of meaningless restrictions."

It was customary for babies to be wrapped in a cloth and bound with rope, to keep their arms and legs straight. The baby, wrapped up like a cocoon, could not move at all. There were two reasons for this practice. First, parents believed it helped the baby's legs and hands from becoming crooked. And second, they thought it would teach the baby to become an obedient individual with good manners. Zadi had not been wrapped in ghondagh, and she did not want to restrict her daughter by binding her with cloth and rope.

Zadi was overjoyed to have become a mother and felt blessed to have a beautiful daughter. She had been in the hammam for more than eight months, and she had come to know its secrets, the reason for its existence. Heeding Khanoum Mina's advice, she decided to leave the hammam once her baby was born. "Take everything you have and go, Zadi," Khanoum Mina said. "A timely tear is better than a misplaced smile."

Khanoum Mina also thought it timely for an oath of silence.

"Take what you have seen to your grave, Zadi," she warned. "Nothing should be said about what we have witnessed here. Better not talk about it. Better not to even try." Zadi, who had experienced Khanoum Mina's overcaution before, promised to keep quiet while secretly deciding to tell her daughter all about it—one day.

Chapter Two

Like the rest of the world, Zadi had watched the revolution in Iran unfold, each new word spread on the streets leading to more confusion, but also to the beginnings of a new world. It required from its admirers a certain aversion, for it was important to ignore not only what was real and sweet, but also what was missing inside its believers.

Zadi had been raised by her grandmother to be independent and free. She wanted the same kind of freedom she had enjoyed as a child for her daughter. The prevailing political ambiguity and the gradual imposition of harsh Islamic laws that limited women's freedom created a gloomy outlook for Zadi and many like-minded people. She thought she could not subject her child to what was ahead—years of struggle, gender inequality, and oppression. Zadi could foresee, she thought, what was on the heels of the revolution, and what had been brewing before the revolution. It would bring unbearable conditions for her and for her daughter. So she did what she had to do. She took what she had and left the country with her daughter.

. . .

There they were, the two of them, Zadi and little Maryam, sitting in the departures gate at Heathrow Airport. Maryam sat with her legs curled, her head tucked awkwardly into her mother's lap. Zadi had chosen America as their destination for reasons that had seemed to her at the time arbitrary. But as she sat in the airport in London, the words of the poet came back to her.

It is what it is.

"I met her once, you know. In the ladies' toilets at Harrods, 1965." A woman stood before Zadi, pointing to a newspaper on the seat beside her. The paper had been left by a previous traveler.

The woman tapped the photo on the front page. "You should have seen the hairs on her pale English face. I wanted to take out my tweezers and pluck them out one by one!"

Zadi stared at the woman for a long moment, then looked at the headline. "Thatcher to Take It On: Is Britain Ready for Two Women at the Helm?" The woman sat down opposite Zadi and wrapped her long coat around her legs. A crowd of travelers moved around them as the woman continued.

"Pistachio?" The woman offered a bag of nuts from her soft leather case. Zadi wondered if they would be on the same flight. "Look at them," the woman tisked a moment later, referring to a cordial line of English businessmen. "Like watered-down milk, the lot of them. And they call themselves men." She guffawed, the bag of nuts rattling on her stomach.

She tapped the newspaper again. "The old bird hasn't changed, not one bit. Of course, she had to become a man in some ways. You don't get to where she is without losing some of your feminine charms." She paused, smiling at Zadi. "First time out of Iran?"

And that was when it hit her. Zadi's face suddenly crumpled, tears welling up in the space of a second. Dropping the pistachios from her hand, she folded into herself and began to cry. Her little one began to whimper.

The woman nodded and handed them each a handkerchief from the inner layers of her long mink coat.

"I know, sweethearts," she said. "I've been there, too. A few times over." She shook her head at a misty horizon beyond the departures gate. "You have a good cry, and when you're done, you tell me your story. I am Haji. Haji Khanoum. It's the best way to get rid of the poison, you know. To open your mouth and let it all spill out."

Zadi didn't know whether it was the quaintly disgusted look on the woman's face or the pistachios she continued to peck at, but something about Haji Khanoum struck her as very funny. Zadi burst out laughing, in the middle of her tears. Wiping her eyes, she blew her nose and pulled Maryam to her chest.

"That's right," Haji Khanoum repeated without taking her eyes off the skinny English businessmen. "Tell me, where are you going to? America?" Haji Khanoum smiled, as though she knew the answer already.

"I wish!" said Zadi, wiping her eyes again with her handkerchief. "We wanted to go to Iowa, but as you know, the American Embassy is closed, so we decided to go to Argentina, Buenos Aires. Hopefully we can get a visa from there."

Haji Khanoum got so excited that she suddenly leaped to her feet. Then, taking a pen and an empty envelope from her handbag, she wrote down a name and address.

"What a happy coincidence. I am coming from Buenos Aires and will go back there soon. Go to this place. An apartment is available for you to rent. The place called the Anna Karenina."

Haji Khanoum passed the paper to Zadi. Then, with a stare, she looked up at the gate number. She was in the wrong place. She bent down and kissed Maryam on both cheeks.

"I have to go now. See you soon." She hurried away, turning back a couple of times as she went, waving at Zadi and Maryam with a smile.

The Anna Karenina, a beaux arts structure of undetermined proportions, was situated in the center of Buenos Aires. The building surprised Zadi when she first saw it. When she arrived at the door, she initially thought herself lost, or that she had misread the address scribbled by Haji Khanoum on the back of the envelope.

She peered at the rusted brass plaque outside the front door. It said just what was written in abbreviated Farsi on the envelope: the Anna Karenina Building, 1796 Avenida de Florida. She had come to the right place.

The vacant apartment was situated on the fifth floor. Like the rest of the building, the fifth and final floor had been built at the end of the nineteenth century. Its architect, a Monsieur Ballard of St. Germain in Paris, had been an avid drinker of absinthe, a bon vivant of epic avarice. Winding from the lobby, a marble staircase led to the uppermost landing, where a large oak door was encased by a stained-glass partition.

Zadi could not believe she had taken up the woman's offer, forgetting her hopes of getting a visa to America and going straight to Iowa.

Zadi and Maryam rented the room next to the one that had been occupied by Haji Khanoum. A week later, Haji Khanoum returned from her trip, draped in her mink coat and carrying a parcel. Before Zadi saw her, she heard her cheerful voice and the familiar and unmistakable laugh.

Yes! She is back, thought Zadi, smiling joyfully.

Zadi liked her apartment and her neighbors, but she still wanted to get to America as soon as possible. She applied for a visa from the American Embassy in Buenos Aires and waited for an interview. It took almost a year for the interview to be granted, and then it was without success. She could not fulfill the requirements of the embassy. To secure a visa, one must be a resident of Argentina, have a permanent job, and own property, none of which she could comply with.

After the embassy rejected her application, it took three months for Zadi to decide what to do next.

Why am I going to America, to Iowa? she asked herself. *Do I want to go to see David?*

He had told her in Hamedan that he was from Iowa.

But where is he now? Where did he go? Why didn't he say good-bye to me? Why didn't he leave any traces of himself for me? I have his baby. Why didn't he come back to see her? Why should I chase him? she questioned.

She remembered that David had never told her he loved her. She was burning with love for him, not he for her.

He wanted to have sex with me once and leave, no matter if I became pregnant or not. How about his sense of responsibility? Are all American men like him?

These self-talks became her everyday preoccupation, until Maryam's birthday. The girl was now six years old. Zadi had arranged a small party, invited their Iranian neighbors, hung balloons, and baked a cake.

"Where was Maryam born, Zadi?" asked Parastoo.

"In the hammam in Tajrish."

Suddenly Zadi's face brightened with a flash of red cheeks. A revelation? She started talking out loud to herself, unconscious of the presence of the others. "Hammam! Yes, the hammam! I worked there for months. I learned so much. Forget about America and Iowa, Zadi!

"I am going to open a beauty salon, right here, in this room," Zadi declared decisively. It took a few seconds of silence and the noise of a balloon, popped by Maryam, to wake her up and remind her that there were others present.

"Let's call it the Zadi Khanoum Beauty Salon," Haji Khanoum suggested.

"No! No! It is not going to be only a salon. I want to teach beauty. I will teach you all and others. It is going to be like a school of beauty." Zadi remembered that when she was at the hammam, women secretly called the patron, Khanoum Mina, "Khanoum Thatcher." They gave the nickname "Thatcher" to anyone who was very clever and knowledgeable, especially about social and political issues. So Zadi said loudly and with passion, "I will call it the Margaret Thatcher School of Beauty."

It took less than a month to set up a beauty salon. The three women, Zadi, Haji Khanoum, and Parastoo, went to secondhand shops and garage sales and bought a few pieces of essential but high-quality antique furniture, mirrors, and cabinets. Placed together around a beautiful Persian rug, they made the perfect setting in which to kick off Zadi's new adventure.

"Let's start, girls!" said Zadi, putting her hands on her hips and then balling her fists and holding them up in front of her chest with enthusiasm and determination.

Zadi began demonstrating band andazi, using her two friends as models. Haji Khanoum had a fanatical interest in hair plucking and a keen observation of facial hair: whenever she met a woman, the first thing she did was look for any hairs on the woman's face; she would feel an obsessive impetus to grab the woman and pull the hairs out with tweezers. While Haji Khanoum had some experience in plucking facial hairs, Parastoo was completely ignorant. It made her shiver with panic just to think about it.

So Zadi first chose Haji Khanoum as a model to demonstrate the art of band andazi to Parastoo. Haji Khanoum welcomed the free service and enjoyed being a model; she showed no signs of pain, even with Parastoo's repeated mistakes. When it was Haji Khanoum's turn to experiment on Parastoo, however, Parastoo was intolerant. Haji Khanoum was quite smooth and skillful. But for Parastoo, it was rough and painful. She screamed at the top of her voice, threw her head back and forth, pressed her teeth together, and strained her facial muscles.

"No pain, no gain, *joonam!*" said Haji Khanoum with a mischievous smile.

"You are monsters!" Parastoo declared.

"How about you, princess? Were you an angel?" asked Zadi with a loud laugh.

Chapter Three

"It is what it is," Shadi Ghavami announced, tucking her tongue under her upper lip. "Just like our great poet Rumi said. You choose what you believe in and you stick to it, no matter what anyone else says."

"I'm not sure that's what Rumi meant," Zadi replied, moving closer to her own client. Shadi Ghavami was clearly taking the capitalist approach to the mystic poet's words. "*It is what it is.* God is what it is." Shadi Ghavami cringed as the thread pulled on her upper lip.

"Exactly! It's what you want it to be. Ow!"

"Hold still then!" Haji Khanoum stepped back to observe her handiwork. She shook her head. "I tell you, it goes back to that moment. The day we decided as a human race to put all our eggs in that one basket." Haji Khanoum plucked at another patch of hair. "It was all up in the air. No one believed the old priests anymore, all those cults with their blabbering virgins. That moment—that's when it happened. It set in motion everything we are about today." She pointed around the room. "You understand I am talking about the human race now. The one we are a part of."

"You're bordering on blasphemy there, Haji Khanoum," said Zadi, snipping through a layer of curls.

Haji Khanoum's dark-lined eyes stared into the distance.

"I'm a Haji," she said, shrugging. "I have immunity."

Zadi clipped another lock. "You both have it wrong. Rumi is saying that man fundamentally needs to understand that he is being looked after. That there is something beyond his own ability to know." She reached over the bench. "To know that he doesn't know, and in doing so, he knows. You know?" She sprayed the aerodynamic curls, locking down the Shirley Temple hairdo. Her client, another salon regular, had an obsession with ringlets. The woman coughed, waving at her face.

"Forget what is right or wrong, good or bad," said Parastoo's henna client, Laleh Maher, shifting in her seat. "This world is crazy to begin with, whatever way you look at it. Besides, we were talking about man. Not wo-man."

Haji Khanoum looked up from her threading. "Not this again!" She groaned. Laleh Maher, who in a past life had led a rebelling army up parliamentary steps, waved for Parastoo to stop applying the henna, then turned to the room.

"Man needs to feel like he's secure, like he's got it all figured out. That's why he came up with the whole idea of God, a separate divinity—'without' not 'within.'"

"The blind man is laughing at the bald head!" piped up a woman, a new client walk-in. Three women who were seated around the glass coffee table laughed and nodded.

Laleh Maher clapped her hands at the proverb. "Exactly! We women, we're different. We don't need answers, just freedom."

She raised her fist in the air. "Give us freedom!" She lowered her fist and indicated for Parastoo to continue with the henna.

"I'd be happy with chocolate," Shadi Ghavami sighed, touching her bare upper lip.

Haji Khanoum nodded. "And a twenty-five-year-old ranch hand, wrapping his legs around my divinity."

"And that is how Hallaj said 'I am God' and told the truth!" One of the customers near the door exclaimed.

The gathered women, many of whom had been strangers to one another until that afternoon, erupted into laughter.

Chapter Four

Soheil Bahrami, nicknamed the Capitan, stepped away from the salon door. He walked back down the corridor, hearing the sound of rising voices against his back, the chattering that reverberated through the walls of the salon most every hour of every day. The Capitan, who liked to take his hourly walks around the octagonal corridor, was used to overhearing the conversations that went on in the salon. Making his way past the kitchenette and the bathroom, he arrived at the other side of the corridor, thumbing the small book he carried with him most of the time. It was the one thing he had brought with him from his youth. He walked down the corridor, thinking of the lines that had woken him the night before.

> *Last night I dreamed that angels knocked*
> *at the tavern door,*
> *they kneaded the human clay*
> *and made it into a chalice.*

They were, of course, from Hafez.

The Capitan rounded the apartment building's corridor and looked up. The sky was shimmering through the glass roof. Reaching up like a steeple, the skylight above the fifth floor was often surrounded by half a dozen pigeons. Unlikely carriers of the subliminal, he thought. He stood beside the glass wall that enclosed the next apartment and leaned in to hear the voices that permeated from the curtained interiors.

The Capitan had come to the city a year ago. Walking the streets, he eventually found the building he had heard about. "They've called it after that book," one of his fellow travelers had told him.

His fellow travelers also told him about the salon on the uppermost level of the building, and the women who streamed in and out of its glass-paneled doors from morning to sundown.

"They're like spiders spinning their webs, my friend," one man had told him. "Laying traps for their prey with their gossamer threads."

He had heard the words in the early morning. Waking into the darkness and scrambling up from the mat, he had quickly looked around the room. His daughter was not yet home from the university. She was home most nights, sleeping on the other side of the apartment, behind the cloth that was pinned to the ceiling.

He surveyed the rest of the room, but his search revealed nothing but the sparse furnishings, his backgammon set, a small pile of books, and the trunk he had brought with him on the ship from Turkey.

The lines of the poem were still running through his mind when he heard his neighbor Haji Khanoum.

He heard her every morning at dawn: her feet grazing the floorboards gently, her soles scraping so softly that he had to strain to hear through the thin wall. He knew, even without seeing her, that she was already deep into her morning ritual.

No one woke up as early as Haji Khanoum, not even the young Sookoot couple, Homa and Reza, across the corridor, although they always went for a walk before Haji Khanoum had ceased whirling. That is when the Capitan would make his way to the kitchenette. With the rising sun splaying on his thin shoulders (warming fruitlessly, doing little to penetrate the specter of sickness, his forever doppelgänger), he waited while Darjeeling brewed in the pot. He then walked back with two cups to stand, courteously, outside Haji Khanoum's door until she had finished.

I have never confessed these thoughts, though I am sure my sad turn as Romeo is the floor's private joke, he thought to himself. *But what of it? I would not let such a secret fly by my own doing. Least of all to my daughter, for whom such a confession would be reason enough finally to do away with me, as she ought to have done a long time ago. But she has a big* ghalb, *big heart, my Sheema.*

I knew from the first day I saw her, thought the Capitan, his thoughts turning back to Haji Khanoum. *I knew that the greater part of my waking days would be preoccupied with the tending of such a goddess. A privilege, yes. An indulgence, most definitely. Stupendously audacious—most definitely bold, as more than anyone I am aware that I do not deserve the station.*

Attendant to such manifesting glory—but as Hafez says,

Eternal is the one whose heart has awoken to love

Very little could faze the Capitan by this (his fiftieth year on and in this world) time. He had endured nearly three decades of imprisonment, had felt the ripple of a thousand moral tales run through his veins. As a young boy in his native Tabriz, he had fallen into a carpet loom of gold and brick-red skeins. The thread had temporarily cut off his breath, propelling him into a torrent of outer-body events, but even that shock was nothing compared with how he had felt the first time he climbed those five flights to the top of the Anna Karenina Building. The land-lord had shown the Capitan into the apartment, telling him he was a lucky man: just that morning a room had become available on the fifth floor. As the Capitan paid his deposit, his eyes caught a movement in his next-door neighbor's window. She was spinning around and around on her bare floor.

The Capitan spent a week trying to find a way to meet his new neighbor. Then he thought of telling the woman across the corridor, the beautiful one with the little girl, about his idea for a poetry circle. He loved poetry and had been involved in poetry gatherings through-out his life.

And so it had begun, first with just the three of them: the Capitan, Haji Khanoum, and Zadi—and of course little Maryam. The Capitan, who had the best grasp of the situation, had told each of them to bring their favorite poems, any stanza that was at the tip of their tongues, the first that came to their minds, their hearts; it mattered little what they brought, for the first meetings would be about breaking down barri-ers and getting ready: the *talab*, desire, that comes before *eshgh*, love. Everyone needed to find their rhythm before any order was imposed.

> *Let's know how precious we are for each other*
> *Let's not forget and become oblivious from each other.*

He recited a line from Rumi, and then this:

> *Generous friends give life for their friends*
> *Let's leave our animal nature and be kind to each other.*

Poetry was the reason they gathered at first. Or at least one of the reasons. The other reasons should remain silent, in keeping with the virtue of the hour. But poetry, yes, had brought them together.

And that is how it began to take shape and, gradually, to evolve into something beyond the imagination of the participants. Zadi's place became not only a beauty salon and a school of beauty, but also a gathering place, a sanctuary for women and occasionally for men, a place where neighbors could come together, to talk, about practically anything. A group of Iranians, all with different backgrounds, away from their beloved country, found a nucleus, a hub. They brought news, gossip, ideas, favorite poetry, and, most importantly, their stories. Haji Khanoum, Zadi, Parastoo, and Homa formed a closed circle, in the safety of which they could reveal their most secret lives, while the Capitan and Haji Khanoum built an intimate friendship.

Chapter Five

The poetry nights, after a few trial sessions in which few rules were set, soon became public. They advised all the Iranian residents in Buenos Aires of its existence.

There were the ones from the Anna Karenina, who were always present, but there were others, too. Clients of Zadi's who had heard about the meetings during their salon visits and brought their families, eager to take part in something different yet familiar. Others heard by word of mouth from here and there. They were not like the fifth-floor tenants. They came from other parts of town, and after the meetings, they could leave the fifth floor, go to other parts of the city, back to other lives and spaces that kept their secrets.

Not like the eight who lived on this floor, thought the Capitan. Their secrets were kept, yes, but in entirely different ways.

Everyone was welcome, and so they came, gathering around Zadi's carpet, the smell of crushed henna powder still in the air.

Night would fall through the atrium outside, and the meeting would begin. Someone would start off with a *Zekr*, a remembrance of God. They had not known how to begin, so Haji Khanoum had suggested the Zekr from the Koran to get things rolling. Holding up her palms, she had closed her eyes and recited. "*La Ilaha Il Allah!* There is no god but God!"

Although not religious in the traditional sense, Haji Khanoum had a thorough grasp of the inner workings of the Zekr, that literary impression of the great mystery.

"If there is no god but God, then why are we talking? Why are we here to begin with?" Zadi's little one, Maryam, suddenly exclaimed one night. She had been running about all evening, unable to stay seated next to her mother.

The others who had gathered that night looked around, startled both by the astute observations of the little girl and the audacity of their being gathered in the first place.

Zadi reached out and pulled her daughter onto her lap.

"Because sometimes we need to be told again, my love. To repeat the words so they become an understanding unspoken," she said.

"But if you already know it, then you understand it. 'An understanding unspoken' are just show-off words, in my opinion," replied the little imp, flashing a gap-toothed grin.

She was six years old but small for her age, which made her pronouncements doubly surprising.

> *Our motions at any moment testify to the presence of*
> *God,*

the Capitan recited, winking at the little girl.

Zadi picked up Rumi's book, *The Masnavi*, and read:

> *Just as the turning millstone bears witness to the river's*
> *existence,*

Dust be upon my head and upon my face,
for You are beyond our discernment.

The Capitan continued, while Zadi lightly tapped the tip of Maryam's nose with her finger:

I cannot stop expressing Your beauty,
every moment says let my soul be Your Carpet.

And they laughed. Suddenly, just like that.

So it is with the gathering of like minds—the synthesis is in the light tap, the proclamations of a child that ring out and say yes, somehow in that moment all was right.

Of all the people who came to the poetry meetings, no one surprised Zadi more than Houshang Bahmanian. The young man had come to the Anna Karenina in the winter. He was from the west of Iran, from Lorestan, and had been involved somehow with the revolution, with some students' uprising, although he now worked at a staid job as an accountant. He was a revolutionary, a radical. Zadi had expected him to bring something Marxist to the meeting, but instead he had produced a book he carried with him everywhere. He had insisted on reading from it, saying there was a lot to learn from the famous philosopher Descartes. The Capitan had not agreed.

"Absolutely not! Only poetry for these meetings!" the old man had declared when Houshang pulled out *The Meditations.*

"Who said?"

"I said. We all said."

"Who are you to say what poetry is? The dissemination of reality. The expansion of the mind, the understanding of understanding, it's all here. It's what life is about!" Houshang waved the volume over his head.

"It's not poetry!"

"Who said? Who are you to make the rules? Descartes is poetry as much as any Hafez or Rumi," Houshang countered, standing up.

The Capitan turned to Zadi, a grimace on his face.

"There was never a need for this when I was in jail, part of the brotherhood of cell mates," the Capitan said.

Zadi took a moment before replying. "It seems to me this is a matter of taste. Semantics," she said, nodding to Haji Khanoum to pour the tea. "Maybe we could have both?"

"It's not poetry, I tell you!" the Capitan pounded his knees. His daughter next to him looked as though she might reach out to him, but then sat still, watching. The others in the circle also sat silently.

"Who are you to say what poetry is?" Houshang repeated.

"Poetry is poetry. One knows it when one hears it. It's not the ranting of some crazy philosopher, that is for certain!"

"Poetry is everywhere," Houshang said, tipping up his chin.

"Yes, yes. Like the air and water and Lenin's left foot. All those cockamamie theories of yours," the Capitan exclaimed. "But have you felt anything, young man? Really bled for something that is right? For love? Eh?"

He pounded his chest, breaking into a loud cough.

For a moment it had seemed as though Houshang was about to leave the room, but he turned back instead, helping the old man onto his place on the carpet. Haji Khanoum handed them each tea, and they all drank in silence.

Houshang had also brought a poetry book of Saadi's *Golestan—The Rose Garden*. After tea, he grabbed the book and began reciting:

> *If the bat doesn't want to unite with the sun,*
> *it will not reduce the beauty of the sun.*
> *I lost the time of union and man is ignorant*
> *of the value of enchanting life before adversity.*
> *Slay me. For to die in your presence*
> *is more sweet than to live after you.*

He even closed his eyes while reciting the poem, his hands on his knees, spreading his fingers as the couplets reached feverish denouement.

He opened his eyes, pushing back the small glasses perched on his nose, a subtle tremble in his hand. Yes, he had been a surprise.

The Capitan grabbed the book from Houshang and said, "Now that you are talking about union, of course between two—lovers and beloved—let me read a poem Saadi wrote about the union of mankind, unity, oneness." And he opened the book and read:

> *Human beings are members of a whole,*
> *in creation of one essence and soul.*
> *If one member is afflicted with pain,*
> *other members uneasy will remain.*
> *If you've no sympathy for human pain,*
> *the name of human you cannot retain!*

"So beautiful!" said Haji Khanoum. "Do you know that this poem has been inscribed on the United Nations building?"

Everyone knew and was proud about it.

"That is the unity we hopefully will have here between us," said the Capitan, glancing at the participants for approval.

Following his first meeting, Houshang returned to the poetry nights, but without the book of Descartes. Neither he nor the old man mentioned their argument, neither there nor when they passed each other in the corridor. Both understood that something special was about to unfold in that room, something too precious to be disturbed by—what had Zadi called it?—a matter of taste. Semantics.

No one, not even argumentative Houshang Bahmanian, wanted to disturb that kind of silence.

The Sookoot couple was always present but hardly ever recited. They had come to Buenos Aires the summer after the revolution. They were both in their early thirties, although beyond Homa's close circle of friends in the salon, no one really knew for sure. The Sookoots didn't talk much of their personal affairs. They hardly talked at all, except in passing in the corridor or the small communal kitchenette and bathing room. They occupied the apartment next to Houshang, who had also arrived in the summer, although earlier by two months. In their small room they set up a little studio where they painted miniatures, which they sold at the local weekend market near the president's rose-colored palace. Homa was a plain-looking, nervous woman who kept her eyes glued to her clasped hands or the tray of sweetened breads in the center of the carpet. She was the last person anyone in the circle would have expected to yell out during a poetry reading. They were talking about passion. Homa and Reza Sookoot had remained silent as usual. But on this night, something different happened.

> *I've swept the stairs to the roof*
> *and I have washed the windows too.*
> *Someone is coming,*
> *someone is coming,*

Zadi recited, closing her eyes, her voice rising,

> *someone is coming,*
> *Someone who in his heart is with us,*
> *in this breathing is with us,*
> *in his voice is with us.*

She paused.
"So beautiful! Tell us who is coming, Zadi," Haji Khanoum said.
"Someone who in his heart is with us."
"Yes! Someone is coming!"
"Yes!"

The *yes* had come from her left—it was Homa Sookoot. Homa's eyes were wide. Beads of sweat had risen on her forehead.

The circle fell silent. Then little Maryam said,

> *Yes, soon the door will be wide open,*
> *and my beautiful lover will come in.*
> *Yes, spring is coming to the garden,*
> *and new branches will give blossom.*

The outburst was completely unexpected. Homa Sookoot rarely went beyond a perfunctory greeting if you came across her in the hallway or out on the boulevards. As for the poetry nights, she usually abided by the etiquette of the gathering and contributed enough in her own quiet way, but to say she was meek would be putting it mildly, thought Zadi. Homa's husband, Reza, contributed more to the meetings, bringing the occasional poem, but not often. At the very first public poetry night, it had been established that there would be few rules imposed; there was nothing to say that anyone had to recite. Still, the Sookoots were unusually reticent; they were even quieter than Sheema Bahrami, who picked her recitations sparingly but then spoke them with such intensity it usually left everyone speechless for a few minutes.

Homa Sookoot's yelling out, and in such an affirmative voice, was certainly an occasion. It came as a surprise to everyone, no one more so than Homa herself.

She couldn't believe she had done it. Had she really said *yes* out loud?

Yes, she had. What was she thinking of?

She knew exactly what she was thinking, and so did Reza. No one said a thing about it during the meeting, but Homa still thought it prudent to explain her outburst. The next day, she stayed behind when Reza went to the market and knocked on the salon door. There were two clients inside, but they were about to leave.

Haji Khanoum stopped what she was doing. "Homa! Just the woman we need! What do you think of the Queen of Sheba, eh? Do you think she should have shaved her legs for old Solomon?"

"Oh—I don't know." The question caught her off guard. She stood uncomfortably by the door.

"Mind you, we wouldn't have much to do here if she hadn't." Haji Khanoum laughed and waved Homa in.

Chapter Six

"Have you ever been in love, Haji Khanoum?" Parastoo Etemadi asked.

Haji Khanoum stopped what she was doing and looked around the room. "Well, you all know I was married . . ."

"Several times," Shadi Ghavami interjected.

"Yes, several times. Thank you!" Haji Khanoum snipped a length of thread from a large spool.

"So it was love, right, Haji Khanoum?" Parastoo looked at her hopefully.

"In love? Every time, *ma chérie*, every time." Haji Khanoum waved her hands in the air. She paused. "No. Just once."

"Once is enough," Shadi Ghavami said.

"More than enough," said the other customer.

Haji Khanoum shook her head. "No, you're wrong! Never enough. No, never enough."

Once the two clients had left and the salon was clean, they all sat down on the carpet: Zadi, Homa, Parastoo, and Haji Khanoum, who prepared to continue her story.

"His name was Jalalladin Ansari and I was fifteen. His coming to me was like a dream, at a time when I needed dreaming more than anything. I would shake the dust from my coat, and rise. But the story of my one, and the only one, really begins a few years earlier, on the day of my ninth birthday, in the year of 1931. The year my father left for his pilgrimage to Mecca.

"My mother had been gone a year by then. She had left both of us, gone to Europe. She traveled to Europe two times a year, to Paris in the spring and to London in the autumn. That was when the best collections came out, the seasons of fashion and beautiful people. They were beautiful like a stone-faced queen is beautiful, all skinny and white, covered head to toe in the skins of dead animals. That is how my mother dressed most of the time, wrapped in furs, her face so full of powder that the down on her cheeks looked like the wool of an angora sweater.

"I was never close to my mother. If it hadn't been for the stretch marks on her hips—jagged, silvery lines that she would spend hours scrutinizing in front of her vanity—I could have sworn that she had never given birth to me. That was the only time in the day I would spend with her, while she was staring into her vanity mirror. She would finish with her rosewater and goat's milk bath and sit down, brushing her curly red hair.

"It was the exact color of saffron, that hair of hers, dyed with peroxide in a Western-style salon, not like the henna we use here. Cut like the dancing girls in her British fashion magazines.

"Every day after school, I would climb the marble stairs up to the third floor, where her bedroom and boudoir were, and quietly sneak into the steamy bath. I'd take a seat on the gold-and-cream Louis XIV chaise longue at the far end of the room and watch her brush out her short, flaming hair. When she finished with her one hundred strokes—always a hundred, because she believed that number would make it grow thick every night—she would flick her eyes up to me in the mirror and smile. 'Is your *maman* pretty today, Nikki-jan? Am I the prettiest maman in all of Shiraz? Go on, you can tell me the truth. We can keep a secret, you and I. And how did you like school today? What kind of shoes was Khanoum Anvari wearing in your arithmetic class? Did they look expensive? Pointy or round toes, would you say?'

"I am never bitter when I think of my mother. She had a certain standard to uphold, I suppose, being the wife of Shiraz's new police chief. The Shah had appointed my father from his inner circle of confidants, men who had been at his side when he marched into Tehran and threw the Qajar king off his throne. The Shah wanted everyone in the country to dress and act like they were on a film set, something out of a gangster movie. The men all in three-piece suits, the women in silky dresses and black high-heel shoes.

"It was absolutely cuckoo, when you think about it. These were people who for thousands of years had worn baggy pantaloons and tunics with no sleeves, the women in long patchy skirts and every last one of them with a *rusari* wrapped around her braided hair. And here was this new Shah telling them that if they left their houses with their heads covered in scarves, they would be thrown in jail! Can you believe it?

"Of course, my mother loved the new styles of fashion coming in from America and Europe. As soon as the New Year's celebrations in March were over, out would come her seven suitcases. Great big alligator trunks. The alligator trunks would be empty when she left for Europe, but always brimming with couture when she came home.

"Bias-cut gowns with rhinestone bodices topped off by ermine stoles with beady little eyes. Cream kidskin gloves buttoned up all the way to her elbows, and cloche hats trimmed with peacock plumes.

"The trunks were always full, except for this one time. When she had left for London in late September, she had not taken any of her alligators with her. They were piled up in the guest room where she had left them the previous spring. She was not coming back to Iran. She had left my father and me, left the Shiraz of roses, wine, and song.

"It would be years before I would see her again and ask her why she had gone away. But by then, I had already lost and gained a few times over, and understood the forces of love much more. I would understand myself better as well.

"Do you know how in the story of *The Conference of the Birds*, there is the valley of bewilderment? It is one of the pillars, of course. The bewilderment the birds must experience before reaching final unity."

Haji Khanoum paused, looking at the room before her. Everyone—Homa, Parastoo, and Zadi—was listening eagerly.

"That was how it was for me, the bewilderment, before the morning of my ninth birthday. Most of what happened before that age has no shape at all. No color even.

"Like the way the world looks when I whirl in the mornings. When I am turning on my feet. If I have no core to hold me to the earth, to myself, then I am lost to the world. I can't see a single thing flying past me." Haji Khanoum lowered her arms to her sides. "And that is the way my life was before my ninth birthday, the day I was pricked. Cut sharp.

"That morning was particularly cold, I remember. It was late in the month of January, but even in deep winter, the temperature in Shiraz rarely falls below sixty degrees. That is why the nightingale has chosen that city as its playground. Year-round those birds mate and sing their songs, instead of flying to Africa like their English counterparts.

"My mind was on those nightingales when I awoke. I had been having a nightmare about the birds, something to do with the bedtime story my nanny, Faezeh, had told me the night before.

"Faezeh, God help her, was a kind and gentle soul, but when it came time for handing out smarts, she was probably napping under a walnut tree. She should never have told me that story, something to do with a nightingale bathing in its own blood, before I lay my head to sleep.

"Oh, the awful dream I had! A forest of nightingales, their little green feet tilted up in the air, their delicate chests speared through by long thorns. Me screaming, running naked through this dark wood, rained on by the blood of listless nightingales.

"I woke up screaming and dripping in cold sweat. Sweat dripping down my face, my body, into a puddle under my legs. My bed, a canopy with frilly satin sheets, was drowning me. All I could see beyond the frills and fluff and the cave of feathers were the wide windowpanes across the room.

"Frost had caked them over. The wind could have been rattling them as well, but I couldn't hear it over my own screams.

"'Nikki-joon, whatever's the matter? Aiii! What happened, what ate you in your dreams?'

"She had leaped from her bed, a mat on the floor next to the canopy, and was shaking me by my shoulders like a rag doll. Her thick black braids, tied in multicolored ribbons, flapped about like dressed-up eels. They continued to swing back and forth as she shook me from my dreams.

"Spluttering, I recounted my nightmare, the glassy-eyed nightingales.

"'Oh, but the nightingales aren't dead,' Faezeh reassured me. 'It might be cold outside, but they're still alive, sleeping in their nests.'

"She dragged me to the window seat. Using the heel of her fist, she rubbed out two windowpanes, so we both could see. Outside, the day was just breaking. Petals and leaves swirled about.

"The canal was flowing slower than usual, but everything else around was moving quickly. Even the cypresses and palms along the garden walk were beating crazily against each other in the wind. The way they snapped reminded me of the martyrdom parades during *Ashura*, when the men hit themselves with chains.

"I had only seen the Passion Play once, earlier in the year, sitting at that very window.

"My mother had strictly forbidden me to watch the commotion in the street, the *ta'ziyeh* that sent grown men to cry for Hussein, the grandson of the Prophet Muhammad, but I had snuck up to her bedroom while she was having her milk bath and saw the line of black chanting and swaying on the avenue beyond the garden walls.

"The way those chains tinkled, and then went silent in the air before landing on broken skin, is a sound that stays with you forever.

"The pomegranate trees were making a different sound. Although sturdier than the others, they had fared no better. All their fruit had fallen to the ground, the last of the season.

"Faezeh was right; the two birds, Leili and Majnoon—I had named them after the famous lovers in Nizami's book—had made a new nest of twigs in the hollow under the pomegranate bushes. I had made friends with those two birds in early autumn, just around the time my mother left for London.

"'In a few minutes, Leili and Majnoon are going to wake up and sing you a birthday tune, Nikki-joonam.' Faezeh's fat cheeks puffed in and out with excitement. 'It's your ninth birthday, you little monkey! Today you become a woman!'

"She laughed and wrapped her arms around me, burying me in her large breasts. Faezeh was a *Ghashghai*, a tribal person. At night when we were alone, she would tell me stories of her people, the family she had left behind. 'You can never get away from where you belong, little one,' she would say.

"'Now, enough of this nonsense,' Faezeh said, pulling me away from the window. 'We must get you ready. Your aunties are coming today to take you out for your birthday.'

"My aunts were my father's sisters, two cruel women. I never liked them and knew they cared much less for me.

"'You should send her to boarding school, Ephram,' they would say whenever they would visit. 'She's like a monkey, running wild here. Just look at her shoes, her hair.' My father would only grunt, not bothering to look up from his newspaper.

"When I heard Faezeh say that my aunts were coming, darkness came over me.

"'Do I have to see them?'

"'What kind of question is that?' she pulled my birthday dress, a monstrous lace thing, over my head.

"'But why?'

"'Because they are your family. They are going to give you many presents today.'

"But I could see that Faezeh could not convince herself.

"There was a spot under her left eye that always trembled when she got upset. It was doing a wonderful tarantella at that moment.

"She pulled on my lace dress and took me to see my aunts.

"Perhaps Faezeh was right, I thought. My aunts had been most pleasant all day. They had taken me to some of the fancy shops in the bazaar, and bought me a big ice cream cone.

"They also took me to a beauty parlor, a new place specializing in Western styles and treatments. I needed a proper haircut, they said. The hairdresser cut my hair, which was usually plaited into one long braid, into a short bob just like my mother's.

"I was so excited. But there was an empty feeling in my stomach when I showed my father.

"'Baba! Look! Look what I got!'

"I turned around in my lace dress, my new hair shifting against my chin. My aunts had left by then, returning me to Faezeh's care. She was standing next to me, biting her lip.

"My father got up from the dining room table, where he was reading his newspaper. He came around to stand before me. He towered over me, and I remember him leaning down so that his face was right in front of mine.

"He slapped me.

"'Never let anyone touch your hair,' he said, and walked back to his seat.

"I ran upstairs before Faezeh could reach me and entered my mother's boudoir. The room had been turned into storage, but her vanity mirror was still there, covered with a blanket. I took it down and stood before the mirror. I stared at my new hair and clothes. The bob looked pretty and sharp, different against my lace dress.

"My father's slap was rising on my cheek. It was a dark, red mark.

"I blinked. Something was moving in the mirror. I blinked again. She kept standing next to me, just an inch, maybe two, away. I moved to the right a bit, but that person stayed still. Then very slowly, she moved to stand next to me again.

"She had the same haircut as me. The same red face.

"I did not look in that mirror again."

Chapter Seven

Sheema Bahrami watched the evening crowd on the sidewalk below. With her arms folded and her long legs crossed, she was a startling, imposing figure against the columns of the university building; her lab coat, her short dark hair, and all six feet of her were as unlikely a combination as Doric columns in the Southern Hemisphere. Or perhaps that was her ego, her *nafs*, talking. Perhaps it was making her think such thoughts.

From outside, the Santa Maria Central Hospital was a hunk of limestone and gothic peepholes. Inside, the hospital was even more tomblike. Lights flickered along corridors that were no longer in use, and had not been for a long time.

The hospital had already been declared defunct by the government when Sheema had started her studies. The third floor, which housed bedridden patients suffering from various maladies, had only recently been reinstated, especially for the students at the university. When Sheema had told Helen what was happening at the hospital—the unannounced visits from the militia, the routine interrogations—it had given Helen even more reason to leave Buenos Aires.

"Just think of it," Helen had said. "Taking the river, the pathway. The motion of moving on, pushing through the waters."

She was going back to the Amazon and to the project that had brought her to South America in the first place.

"They're going to need doctors," she said. To which Sheema had remained silent.

"Tell him you are going to help save love, the root of all those poems," Helen told her when Sheema had mentioned her father. "He'll understand."

But how could she tell her father, who wanted something else? Whose idea of love was so different?

Who would have thought things were only beginning between her and Helen, when they were in fact ending?

They had first met at a lecture. Sheema had been running late from her previous class on Barrio Norte, where most of the university was situated. Pushing breathlessly into the hospital auditorium, she saw the woman standing in front of the lectern, a pot of orchids in her hands.

Helen was talking about the effect of photosynthesis on plant life. What happens when a plant encounters the sun's rays? It breathes, releasing oxygen into the air.

As Sheema caught her breath, Helen's words came at her like rushes of light.

"First. Last. Inner. Only that breath. Breathing human being." Helen touched the orchids lovingly. "Root to stem, the water makes its way up. Opens the petals. Unifies them with the sun. With light. With the greater divine."

Sheema could feel herself trembling. She had never heard a Westerner refer to Rumi before. Helen continued, "The Sufis, those heretical men of Islam, practice their belief in the power of the Beloved by turning. In a dance." Helen clasped one of the orchid stems. "With one hand lowered to the earth's core and one hand lifted to the sun, they pay tribute to God by going around and around." Her fingers spiraled up the thick stalks.

"Breathing in and out, in remembrance of the source that connects us all." Helen spread her open palm above the flower. "Breath. The element of love." Helen looked up. "Breathe. Now. Stop thinking. Thinking ruins everything."

Sheema had never met anyone like Helen. Helen was an ecologist helming a project in the Amazon and had come to the university as a visiting lecturer.

That Sheema had been bestowed with Iranian culture made her a natural source of inspiration in Helen's universe.

Sheema felt like a tiny shoot—a light, living being—whenever Helen brushed her with her lips or laid her long hair on Sheema's bare chest. She became as essential as breathing for Helen.

Helen had only been in the city a few weeks, but already she knew the places to go, the streets to be in. There were corners Sheema had never known existed, secret gardens and cafés where they would sit, talking and drinking wine and *mateh*, the bitter tea of the locals. Bandoneon musicians would play, never batting an eyelash when Helen guided Sheema along the dance floor. Sheema would feel burning hot and awkward for her lack of coordination, the long legs she did not know where to put, the arms that seemed to jut out of her, heading nowhere.

But with Helen Dwyer she never had to look over her shoulder, never had to whisper when walking into a room, afraid that her awkward body and voice would disturb the firmaments. With Helen she could be reckless yet cosseted.

And that was what she was going to tell her father. Tomorrow, after the poetry meeting.

Her father had come to Buenos Aires before her, boarding the ship from Ankara, Turkey. He had insisted on going first, to get established.

He had gone to Ankara from Iran after being released from jail. Sheema had found him waiting in the doorway below the small room she had shared with her mother after separating from her husband the previous year. Her mother had died six months prior from a sickness; she told her father this as they stood in the alcove.

He asked her about her husband. The streets of Ankara echoed with such things; everyone knew everyone's shame. All that shame built up. She had grown terribly thin, her tall frame bony, her cheekbones sunken. Her husband had torn her in the wrong ways. And her father could see all the pain his daughter had gone through.

Chapter Eight

Houshang Bahmanian made his way to the plaza. The streets were quiet, and except for a few figures inhabiting park benches, no one else could be seen. He continued his walk along the pavement, reaching and encircling the war memorial.

I think, therefore I am.

He had discovered Descartes like he had discovered many other things. He had a natural, uncompromising curiosity, a curiosity that did not let him rest once it latched onto a question. He had also developed an ability to account for things, as though in the counting, something was attained beyond what was already there . . . to count was to know. As though with the assignation of a number, an object would take on eternity, reach the divine. That was what capitalism was all about, was it not?

I think, therefore I am.

His people had been of a nomadic sort, traveling through the northern plains of Lorestan, from one end of the province to the next, grazing sheep and goat. What a simple existence, to take only what was needed, to know your place in the machine of things.

When he grew up, he helped his father with the care and the counting of the herd. Now, he had turned this simple skill into a means of making a living.

I think, therefore I am.

Then she must be Zadi Heirati, he told himself. Because she was all he ever thought about.

I think of her, therefore I am.

The palm trees in the plaza swayed as the sun came up over the presidential building. He had a few hours to himself each morning, before heading downtown to his job at an international accounting firm.

Every day, he worked in a large room with many other people, separated like rabbits by partitions, typing on large calculators, filling in column after column of meaningless figures. As he worked on the automated machines, his mind was on Descartes, or more often than not on Zadi.

He had first seen her soon after he had moved into the building. She had been standing on a stepladder, changing that infernal light bulb on the wall near the oak door.

He would see her preparing for her day in her little salon: spinning the thread, polishing the mirrors, reaching out for a book to flip through before anyone else arrived, a smile of understanding on her face.

The way she held herself: her eyes looking out beyond what was before her.

She was a goddess. Not his equal, he knew. He had tried to tell her this one day, but it had come out all wrong. Without the words of another, he was hopeless, it seemed.

He had known girls at university, good, healthy girls with the fire of the cause in their marrows. But no one made him feel like Zadi. To look at her was to look at divinity. A woman like that. To have come all this way, to fight for what she believed. With an ongoing push inside her—she was urged to do something, to create something good, to get to a place she knew was there on the horizon but that she had yet to grab . . . reach . . . God!

A woman like that made you believe in just about anything.

She made him feel desire, possession. He felt that possession, the state of it, as though it was a possession. Never before had he understood what it meant to be Majnoon, a madman in love, like in the poem by Nizami. He wanted to possess her as she possessed him.

She thought she could hide her struggle, her pain, but he saw right through it. And to the other side.

On his fifth turn of the plaza, Houshang saw for the first time the mothers, the Madres de Plaza de Mayo. They were beginning to congregate at their usual spot beneath the memorial, holding up their banners, their white shawls with their children's names woven across them. They gathered there every Thursday, looking for their children, who had been taken by the militia.

He had told Zadi about the mothers. She had heard about them, but she had never seen them gather in the plaza. How he would like her to see them.

Houshang averted his eyes as he walked past the group of white kerchiefed women. He felt guilty watching them. They moved around the memorial as though they were in Mecca, with their placards and banners. Maybe they really did believe that they were going to find their lost children, or maybe their need for the physical had been superseded by something that was unspoken.

Why, life?

Why so impossible?

The thing that got to him, that had attracted him to the revolution, was that internal turn within a person—what happened to people when they began to revolt, to change from within, and to become something else. That was why he loved poetry. What really drew him to the words. He understood those lines that called to him. Revolt, the turn in a turn.

Houshang Bahmanian stood in the salon doorway.

"Ladies. Hello, hello!"

He looked slightly embarrassed. His hair was disheveled, and there was excitement in his voice. He looked at Haji Khanoum. "Have you been watching your television, Haji Khanoum?"

"Not today," Haji Khanoum replied. "What's the news, gorgeous?"

Houshang shook his fist, his voice cracking. "It's happening! It's happening!"

Parastoo, frightened, stopped clipping. "What do you mean?"

Her client turned around. "That's right. I heard it's happening."

Zadi turned to Houshang. "What's going on?"

"It's another war, Khanoum Heirati. The British are invading the islands. Margaret Thatcher and her army."

It was true. The television in Haji Khanoum's parlor apartment, a space that was also used for the salon's longer treatments, confirmed the news: the imminent arrival of an army from Britain. Though no one could make much headway as to the why or how of the matter.

Haji Khanoum shook her head as she pulled on Narges Tapesh's chin. "I hope she finally did something about that facial hair of hers."

Everyone stared at Haji Khanoum. She shrugged. "It's a long story." She gave Zadi a knowing smile.

Houshang nodded. "In that case, I have got to go. I'm getting back to the plaza. It's all happening!"

The Capitan, who had been standing in the corridor, grimaced and shook his head. "No respect. Where is your sense of propriety?"

"Propriety is for the feeble-minded bourgeoisie," replied Houshang, and hurried way.

The Capitan looked after him in disapproval. "Bourgeoisie!"

"I don't understand," said Narges Tapesh.

"Exactly!" Haji Khanoum said, shaking her head. "Exactly, Narges-joon."

And she pulled at another hair on her client's chin.

Chapter Nine

Zadi, when she had finished a band andazi, went to the special perfume shelf, picked up a small jar, and sprayed it onto her client. A heavenly perfume called *Ehsaas*—Sensation. The perfume particles spread quickly throughout the salon, stirring up a vivacious and sensuous feeling, transporting everyone to a pleasant spiritual realm. They all forgot about what was happening outside, the news, the war, what Houshang had said.

"This is really the essence of life," said Parastoo, who seemed to have become *mast*, drunk, from the perfume.

This elevating atmosphere reminded Zadi of her grandmother.

When Zadi was seven years old, her grandmother—a sensational beauty—had shown her the meaning of her essence. The unmistakable power of it.

"Discover it," her grandmother, Shahrzad, used to say, "and you can never be fooled by anyone. Never be led by the selfishness of their desires. Discover your essence and you can go anywhere you like, be anything you want, Shahrzad-jan."

The summer had come and gone quickly that year. Her parents had died in June. They had been asleep when gas had leaked into their bedroom, killing them quickly and silently. Although to hear Zadi's father's sister tell it, it was as if her parents had asked for it.

"She had her fingers in his hair, as if she was combing it. Can you believe that?" her aunt had exclaimed.

The image had stayed with Zadi all throughout the summer: her young mother lovingly holding the head of her beloved, claiming it, soothing it, in an act that was proprietary and purposeful, as though she really were combing her husband's dark hair, preparing him to face whatever was to come.

The thought had comforted Zadi, even if the intention of her aunt had been to do the opposite. It was no secret that her father's sisters were not happy about Zadi coming to live with them at her grandmother's house in Hamedan.

Her essence. She was soon to discover it, and to begin to see the beauty in things. In nature herself.

It was after her parents' funeral. Grandmother Shahrzad had left her to discover the rest of the house. Zadi had wandered out to the orchards and the outer walls, which were covered with morning glory. It was a beautiful orchard, but Zadi was too sad to do much but sit under the persimmon trees, staring at the blades of grass. Her mind was so full of sadness it was almost empty.

And that was how Grandmother Shahrzad found her.

"Are you ready to see a place of magic, little one? A place filled with light?" Grandmother Shahrzad was grinning at her. She was wearing her chador and favorite rusari, the one she wore only on important errands. "Well, what do you say? Ready to come down to earth for a while before being lifted up again?"

Without waiting for an answer, her grandmother had pulled Zadi into her arms. Moments later they were walking out of the estate's green gates, to the trolley stop on the street corner.

The trolleys were still pulled by horses in Hamedan then, although Fords and Paykans roared down the new highways. Her grandmother was too practical for automobiles.

"They are the beginning of the end for our country," she would say. "Even if everyone else thinks otherwise. You see, little one, the speed of the body—for that is what cars are, really, the speed of the atoms in your body, rattling like bullets against your being—the speed of the body leaves no time for the knowledge of God in your soul. How can you, with all that sound and air rushing past you?" Grandmother Shahrzad had smiled. "And the same thing goes for your essence."

"Where are we going, Maman Bozorg?" Zadi had to skip to keep up with her grandmother's strong legs.

"No questions, *joon-e man*. Not yet. Just silence. Just follow the silence. It will lead you down all the right paths, sooner or later."

And her grandmother continued her strident pace.

There was no silence on the streets of Hamedan, and certainly not on the trolley they took from outside the estate. Zadi remembered how she held her little ear out the trolley window, thinking she would get an answer, but she could only hear horses, merchants yelling their wares in the bazaar, and the wail of prayers from the mosque. Her grandmother had said they were going to a very special place, a place of magic. All Zadi knew of magic was from the cinema, the Disney films playing in the movie theater. There was Dumbo the flying elephant and Pinocchio with his nose getting longer by the minute. Magic was American. Nothing she saw on the streets outside the trolley window was magical in any way.

But where her grandmother took her was no ordinary street. It was another place, a place of magic.

They stepped out of the trolley. Grandmother Shahrzad patted Zadi's hand.

"You know the story of Ali Baba I told you," Grandma Shahrzad said. "The story with the cave and forty thieves? Well, imagine the forty thieves decided to retire and become merchants instead. No ordinary merchants, but merchants of magic. Magic smells." And that is what that street was, where the trolley let them off. They were in the Alley of the Anointed, her grandmother said, taking Zadi's hand.

Anointed meant oil. The oil that was sold in ten or so shops tucked into one lopsided street just off the main throughway. Each shop in this alley had a specialty, a scent for which it was best known. Although a person could technically buy any essence in any shop in the Alley of the Anointed, you would have to be an amateur or a tourist to do so. If you wanted frankincense, for example, you would go to Khoroush the Kurd. He had a cousin in Eastern Kurdistan who ground the golden resin himself in a large brass basin.

All this Grandmother Shahrzad explained as she led Zadi by the hand down the alleyway. They passed the vendors—each shop the same but with minor variations, the arrangement of jars or the calligraphy of their name slightly different in some way—and kept on until they were midway down the lane. Then, stopping before a shop like all the others—that is to say, dusty and stacked with clear vats of multicolored oils—they stepped inside.

The man behind the counter was also of no special breed. He looked entirely the same as all the other vendors, although older than some, perhaps: some teeth were missing and his nose was large enough to take in and reject any unnecessary particles. He hardly blinked but kept polishing the large glass vats behind him with a silk handkerchief.

They stood in front of that perfume merchant in the Alley of the Anointed for what seemed like a very long time—maybe five minutes, maybe half an hour—until he had moved over all the vats with that silly handkerchief of his. Those oils! The color of gemstones, Zadi thought. Ruby and cobalt. Ambers of all shades. A green like the pine of the Alvand Mountains in Hamedan. Strange enough, however, there was no definite smell to the shop itself. It was as if those vats allowed no escape. Even the smell of the oil would have cost you, Grandmother Shahrzad would say. "Nothing is for free. Remember this, little one," she said.

When the man finally turned to them with his blank expression, Zadi fully expected him to ask them what they wanted to buy. Instead, he cocked his head, stared into her grandmother's eyes and said, "*Ya-Haqh*, Haji Khanoum." Oh God, the truth, the right. It was a sign of respect, especially among tradespeople, to call an older man Haji Agha and an older woman Haji Khanoum; *Haji* referred to someone who had gone to Mecca to pray, to pay their respects and their religious duty.

"Ya-Haqh, Haji Agha," replied Grandma Shahrzad.

So that was it. The cost was simple yet priceless. With that, the perfumer showed them into a hallway, to a door carved from heavy walnut. All Zadi remembered was that one moment everything was dark, and then the cedar door opened to reveal a glass ceiling, a room filled with the smell of goodness. Of virtue.

"You see, little one," Grandma Shahrzad said, leaning down to Zadi's awed face. "I have brought you to a place of true beauty. The place where everything goes after dying."

Before them stood two hundred or so globes the size of ripened cantaloupes. Each one was made of glass, with a fluted neck that rose to attach itself to a pipe of clear crystal. The pipe ran along a wall to a vat the size of a small pool at the end of the room. In every globe was a tonic of shimmering pink liquid, over which floated a coverlet of petals. Rose petals.

"Like the soul rising from the body, the petal essence is drawn out. It then gets taken into those vats, and is chilled and perspired. What remains is the diamond of smells. It is that which Haji Agha here puts into his jars. That is why we wait. What makes the rosewater so precious."

Grandmother Shahrzad straightened her back and nodded at the old perfumer. "That is the magic. The magic that comes from giving your everything. Always."

As they walked home that evening, Zadi's grandmother told her the rest of the roses' story. "What remains, Zadi-jan. What remains is important. Like those roses, you must wait. Sit still and wait until all those parts of you that have no purpose fly up. Until all you can hear, all you can see is your essence, your atr."

And that is what she did. They returned to her grandmother's house, and Zadi returned to the persimmon tree. And there she sat. She sat until nighttime, until the next morning. Not once did her grandmother Shahrzad disturb her. She knew as well as Zadi what was happening. Zadi sat until the next afternoon's sun came through the leaves. She thought of those petals, how the rose willingly gave over the parts that were seen, the beautiful parts.

Every time she felt one part of her was fighting the other, she thought of those petals giving way. And soon enough, Zadi, too, was calm.

All that was left as the night came, once again, was the quiet. And the knowing of how.

For Zadi felt it then, her atr, her essence, as she sat waiting under the persimmons. She felt it in her stomach, in her heart and head, all at once. She let the feeling take over her completely. She wanted to store it up in her memory forever.

This knowledge did not leave Zadi. For many years it stayed with her, even as she grew into a young woman. Until the year she turned eighteen and everything changed—even her essence.

Chapter Ten

Parastoo sat down on a chair, still flying through the air of drunkenness from the perfume. She, to the shocked surprise of everyone, loudly recited from Rumi:

> *Oh my beautiful, today I don't see us divided*
> *I am so drunk that I can't find my way home.*
> *In this love, I departed from reason*
> *I don't know but madness and distraught.*
> *They said, there is a hidden bait in this trap*
> *I am so trapped that I don't see the bait.*

They did not think that Parastoo knew things, especially poetry, but she knew. She was not completely ignorant of knowledge and books. Just because she had not attended university and could not recite poetry like the rest of them—and how she envied their ability to do so!—did not mean she was not aware of the beauty of poetry.

She had loved those poems of Hafez and Rumi since first hearing them as a little girl, in her father's tailor shop, or around the dinner *sofreh* after the tea and fruit was served. She had, in fact, memorized the entire *ghazals* from *Kolliyat Shams* of Rumi by the time she was twelve. But no one knew about that. To take those ghazals into memory took a strange nerve, a courage of some sort maybe, but still a strain of madness that was best not told.

> *I am more eloquent than the nightingale, and I crave to*
> *shout, but because of people's envy I've sealed my lips.*

She thought of Jamsheed. She thought of that day he came calling at her parents' home in their little village. They lived in the desert outside Yazd, in the central part of Iran. She remembered she was sitting at her bedroom window, which jutted out of the side of the house above a patch of tomatoes. Even in December, they were still growing. Those tomatoes were so plump and dark in color they were sometimes taken for plums when presented to dinner guests. Parastoo never knew how her mother managed to grow them so lush and tender. The climate of their central desert made the soil unpredictable, but somehow that patch around their stone house was always rich and wet with life.

She remembered how she was sitting at her bedroom window, embroidering the hem of an old skirt with a new pattern, when she saw him. That white suit gleamed and shimmered as it made its way to their modest entryway, which was barred by a crumbling front gate and wall. The gate must have been left unlocked, for she didn't hear a knock. She was in such awe, she remembered, to see him standing there, not four feet away from her seat in the shadow, that she let the needle slip past the hem and right into her finger. A mound of blood quickly rose above her skin, and she sucked at it absently, tasting the metal, still transfixed by the man poised on the doorstep in his white outfit.

"I had seen him for the first time on 15 October 1971. The exact date was not hard to remember. It was the day of the big parade, the celebrations at Persepolis.

"The ruins of white columns outside Shiraz had once been the palaces of Dariush Bozorg, Darius the Great, that bearded emperor of the Persian Empire. Persepolis had once been a sight to behold, I remember being told in school when I was a girl. A place of glory, of marble halls and columns. Rooftops made from pulsing green, the color of a peacock's heart. As a little girl, I used to imagine what it would have been like to be alive then, twenty-five hundred years ago.

"Maybe I would have been invited to the palaces—as a servant or seamstress to the king's harem—and would have to bow at the landing of the great staircase. I might even enter through the palace doors, the Door of All Nations, which opened to the great court.

"And now, twenty-five hundred years later, the country was to see the palace filled with life again . . ."

"The Shah and his Shahbanoo, his third wife, had decided to throw a celebration at Persepolis. A big party. They wanted to remind the rest of the world of the power of Persian light, bring back the memory of the goodness that had started when the prophet Zarathustra climbed his mountain. Everybody knew how important that moment was to the people of Iran, even the Mullahs and their boys, the ones who took to rejecting everything that did not come from their books. Light and dark, good and evil, that was what Zardosht, Zarathustra, had shown them. Before any other religion was a seed in man's mind, he had already given the message.

"The way to live out this spool of life, the way to rule over their blessed land. Good thoughts, good words, good deeds, that is what he had recommended for a proper life. Everyone knew this. But now they were going to be reminded again, to the tune of a multi-million-dollar banquet in a vast plain near the ruins of Persepolis.

"For over a year, every radio and television station reported on the progress, detailing the minute-by-minute construction of the Golden City, the tented paradise shooting up beside those crumbling palace columns. Not a day went by without a reminder of the coming celebration, which, according to the Shah, would tell the nation of Cyrus and his Babylon conquest. The guest list grew by the day, every royal figure, every dignitary and important being in the world wanting an invitation.

"French designers and French architects, a French chef to orchestrate the banquet. Caspian caviar and Moët champagne were to be served, we were told, and the world's crown heads were practicing their curtsies and Farsi for when they would be presented at the Great Tent. And to top it all off, a parade on the last day, a marching display of twenty-five hundred years of the Persian dynasty. And I was going to be one of the only people outside the guests to see it."

"Although the costumes for the parade were flown in from Paris, local artisans were called on for the finishing touches. Makeup women from the hammams together with seamstresses and tailors, jewelers from nearby villages who knew the right combination of polishes for the headpieces and breastplates were all on hand to corset and shave the actors who were going to take part in the march of the empire. As one of the best tailors in the region, my father had been commissioned by the minister of culture himself, who had requested his needle and thread for any alterations that might crop up before the parade. And I was to accompany him as his assistant.

"I was not my father's first choice for help. My older brother, Sina, his partner in the small business he had set up in our village outside Yazd, had been called up for military service the month prior. I was put under rigorous training to learn all about men's tailoring, a booming industry at that time. Now, no self-respecting Iranian man would wear a tie, that noose of the Western man, but back then ties were the icing on suits that sparkled and flared, strands of silk running through an exact blend of poly-viscose and cotton.

"The morning of the parade, I remember getting up before the sun, with the rooster in our backyard. Driving with my father in his wheezing Packard, which he had bought the year before, we came to the gates of the Golden City.

"No one from the local towns was allowed to enter the gates, to sit and stare at the parade. The people who were getting the party ready, the costumiers and handlers, were masked by large fake columns, made especially to match the real ones on the hill overlooking the vast plain. From there my father would assist the head costumier, a tall, gaunt man from France, and help him with any last-minute stitching. It was there that I first saw Jamsheed, astride his horse, dressed as an ancient Sassanian. He was strapped with golden breastplates, his thick bare arms piled high with cuffs of melted pewter, jewelry around his neck.

"All the men playing soldiers were to look straight ahead, warriors ready to take on the decadence of Babylon, with its hanging garden and Tower of Babel. Jamsheed turned to look at me instead, conquering me in a second with eyes that were smeared with dark kohl and all the wrong intent.

"He came from a neighboring village, but had greater ambitions than our local bazaar stall, he told me later that day, when the weight of the breastplates had three hundred men collapsing beneath the fake columns. The Shah and his guests had retired to their tents, readying themselves for a grand ball later that evening. With three hundred men to tend, my father was too busy to notice a man talking to me. Otherwise he would have surely sent me reeling with the power of his fist.

"'I'm going to Tehran,' Jamsheed explained. 'From there I'll take a plane to New York, make my millions in one, two years, tops.'

"Knowing that questions would make me less than desirable, I held my thoughts and waited for him to tell me how he was going to do this, to make his millions. There was no secret to the seduction of men. Even I, a virgin of seventeen, understood this basic tenet.

"A duck of the head, a lowering of the lashes, a blush here and there, and they will bite like hungry lions. To hold your heart in your throat, to feel a flutter at even the slightest look from a man, to hide. That, my mother had always told me, was what an Iranian woman should be like.

"And it certainly worked on Jamsheed. It took him no longer than a moment of my embarrassed silence to tempt him to spill his secrets.

"With excitement, he pulled out a piece of paper from a rucksack and held it before me. It was yellowing and had creased from the many times he had opened and closed it.

"'This,' he said with all the pompous air of an elite Sassanian, 'this is my ticket to greatness.'

"On the paper was a drawing, a diagram of a large animal. I instantly recognized it as a lizard, like the ones I used to see scurrying across the desert floor, the ones my older brother would often catch and kill, dissecting the poor things with our father's tailor shears. But this lizard was not real: it was a toy, the blueprint for a toy that would crawl along the ground. Jamsheed's ticket to riches, to American millions.

"'It works like a yo-yo,' he explained. 'There is a rolling pin under his body, see, and a string that pulls the pin, unrolling it and rolling it, making the lizard go. All I would need is a few hundred dollars to invest in it. Some paper, some paint, and I am set. The American children have never had such a plaything! It will be bigger than any toy, you'll see!'

"It would be the first of many plans that would never see the light of day. But I didn't know that then. All I could see was the gleam in his eyes, what I took as determination."

Every time you see me, you increase my pain
Every time I see you, I want to see you again

"He smiled again and blinked. 'Did anyone ever tell you that you have beautiful skin? White as the Alborz snow. The desert is no place for you, that is for sure.'

"I remember blushing and ducking those penetrating eyes of his again. It would not be until later that I would find out there was nothing beneath that gleam. Like the breastplate he was wearing, it hid flesh too used to the comfort of its own beauty."

"After that parade, I would often see him in my village. He would come to the square, where there were a few Western-style cafés, and sit all day long, waiting for me to return from my father's shop, where I kept the books in a back room. He would always offer me a tea, but I always refused. My entire reputation would be ruined in the second it would take to sit down at that table with him. Everyone in my village knew me, knew about me.

"I was a virgin, as I ought to be, never courted by anyone. Not in all my seventeen years.

"Maybe Jamsheed knew this. Maybe he could tell even before looking at me on that day at Persepolis. Maybe he had me picked for someone who would only twitter, let him gleam, let him fly, while I hopped around the ground, seeking food, making a nest, surviving. Whatever the reason, he had chosen me. And I had no one in my head but him.

"He finally made his move, a few months after Persepolis. He came to my home one morning, dressed in his three-piece white suit, one he had purchased from my father's shop with a week's earnings. His hair gleamed from Brylcreem, and his sideburns and moustache were trimmed only a little, so as not to appear too modern.

"My father was used to bartering his innate Persian pride for the dollar, but his own daughter was something else. He would never accept a dandy for a son-in-law, a dreamer with no steady qualifications, just a string of odd jobs and a toy lizard for a future. When Jamsheed asked him for permission to take me to Shiraz, to the local discotheque, it took less than a second for my father to shut the door in his face. Then he turned around and slapped me.

"'Whore,' he called me. 'What have you done to me?'

"In my father's mind, I had made Jamsheed come to our door with that gleam in his eye. I had lost my *sharm*, my dignity and femininity, and could never get it back. I tried to tell him the truth—that I had no idea Jamsheed would come calling in such a brazen way, that I had done nothing to lure him—but my father had no ears for it. My version of the story did not matter. Not then, and not later, when I told it again to myself."

Chapter Eleven

Zadi stepped outside the Anna Karenina and turned toward the northern avenue. She had asked the Capitan's daughter for the favor of allowing them a look-see, wanting Maryam to see what it was like to walk the hallways of a proper hospital. Neither of them had ever been inside one, after all.

"Just like the ones we saw in *Doctor Zhivago*, Maryam-jan," said Zadi. They had watched the movie on Haji Khanoum's television set one night last winter. Omar Sharif as the poet doctor, his life ruptured by a revolution. Zadi had seen the film as a young girl, at the local cinema in her hometown of Hamedan.

"You'll be just like Dr. Zhivago," Zadi had said to her little one as they watched Omar Sharif fighting the Cossacks to save a wounded woman. "Dr. Maryam, they'll call you. Dr. Maryam, we need you."

Soon after, Zadi had gotten the idea to take her daughter to the university hospital so she could see real patients, to feel what it would be like to help them.

If anyone asks you about the fairies,
show your face and say, like this!

If anyone asks you about the moon,
climb up on the roof and say, like this!
If anyone asks what there is to do,
light the candle and say, like this.

She picked Maryam up from school, and after a brief chat with one of the teachers, who was among the handful of Argentinean clients who came to the salon, she buttoned her daughter into her peacoat and took her by the hand, leading her westward to the hospital. Sheema Bahrami, the Capitan's daughter, would be waiting for them there.

"Are you excited about tonight, joon-e man? What you're going to see?"

Maryam looked up at her with those big brown eyes. "It's what I've dreamed of, Maman," she said. She wrapped her arms around Zadi, squeezing her face against her stomach.

Zadi's heart swelled. She had watched this tiny being since the moment she first held her in the palms of her hands. She had observed the miniature of her blossoming character. And in that blossoming, she had seen herself, and the things she had understood as a young girl. Had it not been for poetry and the wisdom of her grandmother's words, she could never have grasped those things, for all the wealth in the world: the beauty of things, the intricacies of nature, and the sureties of its seemingly infinitesimal and arbitrary decisions.

She noticed this strange magic everywhere she went. But it wasn't just the beauty of life Zadi had seen as a little girl. For as long as she could remember, she had seen pain. She could see the needs and loneliness of people, just by looking at them. She could be sitting on a bus or walking to school and she would glance at someone, a complete stranger, and see his or her past and future unfold, see their everyday lives come together as one in the same moment. In an instant.

She could see them, in a way that she could not fully understand or explain, even as she tried to explain it to her grandmother Shahrzad one day.

They had been sitting, as they often did in the afternoons, on the back porch, watching the persimmon trees in her grandmother's garden rustle in the wind. Zadi told her grandmother what she had felt, what she could understand when she looked at people. She could tell their stories, their innermost hearts, and the heart at the center of the heart, she said, whispering the secret, as the wind kept on its soliloquy.

"I can see what people want by just looking at them, Maman Shahrzad. How lonely or happy they really are."

Her grandmother had given her a knowing smile.

"There is a word for what you know," she'd said. "Ghalb, the eye of the heart.

"Everything that was mapped out in the human body, in the human heart, it all comes back to that mysterious place. The ghalb with its intention for life, for happiness. No one can see it, but it is there. If any one thing is off balance, it is the ghalb that will take you there, Zadi-jan. To become whole again."

Zadi watched her daughter skip ahead of her, giggling as passersby stopped to pat her on the head. To foster Maryam, to give her every opportunity under the sun, Zadi wanted that more than anything.

It was one of the reasons she had first agreed to the poetry meetings. That and the light she had seen in the Capitan's eyes when he talked of his old poetry circle.

It was that kind of light that had made Zadi look for beauty all those years back.

Sheema watched the lights at the end of the plaza. From the university hospital, you could see the entire eastern end, all the way to the rose-colored presidential palace. All day long, people were gathering in the area. Demonstrators gathered every Thursday, looking for their lost children, but today there were more than usual. She was waiting for Zadi and Maryam.

Zadi harbored dreams of her daughter becoming a doctor of some sort one day—somebody, she said, who could heal anyone by just walking into a room. That was hardly how it worked in real life, Sheema had tried to tell her, but it had fallen on closed ears. Zadi wanted something, it seemed, although it was hard to know what that was, exactly.

And strange as it was, Sheema understood that kind of desire; she too had wanted something all her life without knowing what that something was.

When she was little it was clear to her. She wanted to be with her father, to see him, to sit on his lap, to be hugged and kissed by him. Yes, she wanted her father, whom she had never known, as he had been imprisoned before she was born. She fantasized about and idealized an imaginary father whom she would meet one day.

His touch, the embraces she had imagined receiving as a little girl, had caused her head to spin with joy.

But when he had come to her finally—released, he told her—after the revolution hit the streets of Tehran, he was nothing like what she had expected.

It made her body convulse and react in strange ways. She felt like she was being dispersed, her body shattering into billions of particles, with spaces in between them so that one could not tell if they had ever been part of a whole. She felt that way for days after his return. But after he confronted her about what had happened to her, she did feel a little more real again, except this time all those pieces had been gathered into a dark revolving slump in her center. No story could ever be told.

Sheema was born in Ankara, a few months after her mother escaped Iran fearing persecution; she had been active, supporting her husband's political line.

Missing her husband, her family, her friends, and her country, she had slowly become physically and mentally sick. But for the love of her daughter, she resisted her sickness until Sheema got married.

Haji Mahmoud Nosratollahi, a very religious and influential Mullah who had escaped Iran with his family and had gotten refugee status in Turkey, was supporting Sheema and her mother.

Sheema, having a sick mother and an absent father, slowly adopted a nursing role at home. At school, she was a successful student. But she lacked any ambition for her own future. She became careless about herself.

It is what it is.

After she finished school, she applied for many fields of study at university, including engineering, agriculture, and medicine. She was accepted into all of them.

I don't know which one I should continue to study, but I know one thing, she thought. *I want to be able to cure my mother.* So she had enrolled in medicine.

She had been coming out of a doorway. She was lost—the streets of Turkey were not so dissimilar to the ones in Buenos Aires. She had found herself repeating the words in her head out loud. She did that often, reaching into a well deep within to pull out lines and ghazals that had been placed there by unseen hands, lines that had been there ever since she could remember. She was repeating those words when she saw him.

Alireza, the son of Haji Mahmoud Nosratollahi, was standing in an alcove across the alley. The rain was falling on his face as he stepped out to talk to her. There was a poetry night not far from here, he said, if she cared to join him. She had to help her mother with the sewing, she told him, walking away.

But a few weeks later, he came to the small room she and her mother lived in. He and his father sat down on the small carpet in the living space.

Haji Mahmoud Nosratollahi politely and abstemiously, as is the custom on such an occasion, asked Sheema's mother to accept his son as their servant, *gholaam*, Sheema's husband.

At the time, Sheema was in her second year of medical school. She was not thinking about marriage at all. Sheema and Alireza had grown up together in Ankara, as neighbors and friends. She had thought of him as a good boy; she never saw any major problem with him, so she liked him as a friend, except that Alireza, in contrast to Sheema, who was a moderate Muslim, was very religious and had to follow his father, participating in many religious gatherings and rituals. "I want to finish my degree first. Besides, I have to take care of my maman," said Sheema, feeling shocked by the proposal and suddenly trapped by an inevitable fate.

They said, there is hidden bait in this trap.
I am so trapped that I don't see the bait.

"No, no problem at all. You can finish your degree and take care of your mother. I promise that," said Haji Mahmoud Nosratollahi, smiling with sincerity and innocence. "I promise!"

She caught her mother's eyes, but they contained no secret message. She already knew the secret. Her destiny had been engraved on her forehead from the beginning of beginnings. What else could her sick mother have said to a man who had been so generous and kind, helping her and her daughter during these difficult times?

They never made it to the university hospital. As they crossed the avenue, the mob on the plaza had begun chanting. Death to Margaret Thatcher. Death to the army. Maryam looked at Zadi with frightened eyes as they crossed back to where they had just come from.

They were silent until they reached Calle de Florida.

"Maryam! Joon-e man! It's all right if you were scared." Zadi squeezed her daughter's hand. "It's just silly things. Silly people. We'll go to the hospital another day."

Maryam stared at the pavement, then stopped. She shook her head, her little plaits tapping against her school uniform.

"I don't want to go to the hospital. I don't want to be a doctor. I don't want to be a doctor when I grow up."

"Of course you do. You have never even been in a hospital." Zadi leaned down to look into her little one's eyes. "Remember, you weren't even born in one."

Maryam shook her head again. "I don't want to. I don't want to be a doctor!" She let go of Zadi's hand.

"But it's what you've always wanted!" Zadi poked her daughter with her finger. Just then a thought came to her. She thought to have some fun with Maryam, maybe a game of hide and seek! "Look at me," she said, and she ran toward the apartment building.

She stopped at the Anna Karenina's front door, looking back over her shoulder. Her daughter was still standing halfway down the street.

Zadi turned into the lobby. When she looked back again, Maryam was inside the building.

"Stop it!" Maryam screamed, her hands on her hips.

"I am running away! See!" Zadi ran up one of the long staircases. She entered the fifth-floor landing, stopping to catch her breath.

Opening the door, she stepped into the corridor just as Maryam reached the landing. She laughed, shaking her head. "Don't be such a scaredy-cat!"

"I said stop it!"

Maryam rushed angrily toward the salon's entrance and hit the glass door with her fist so hard that it made a large hole in the beveled glass, a small pane right above the door handle. The pieces of glass scattered on the floor at their feet.

Maryam screamed at the top of her voice, holding her bleeding right hand.

Zadi rushed toward Maryam, trying to calm her while examining her wrist.

All their neighbors came out to observe the shocking scene.

"Hurry up! Take her to the hospital," the Capitan said.

The beveled atrium shone a miracle of color, the birds scattered on its ledge, spilling shadows onto the mosaic floor below. Soon they would head over spires and cathedral tops, over oxidized domes weathered by forces that could be harnessed but never commanded. As Sir Francis Bacon said, the forces of nature could be tamed, as long as one abided by their rules and requirements.

In other words, *it is what it is*, so just get on with it.

. . .

Pausing by the open door, Zadi surveyed the room she had left the night before. The apartment, lit usually by lamps in every corner, was devoid of any light. Taking a few moments for her eyes to adjust to the darkness, she looked around. They were all there: the bookcase and counter and the chairs gathered around them. The cupboards and the small tables along the back wall, above which hung gilt-framed mirrors of various shapes and sizes.

Nearly everything had been cleaned and put away the night before, and it was this fact that made her catch her breath.

Inhaling deeply, she stepped inside. The antique sideboard near the door was wiped clean, except for an open box of henna powder, which sat partially overturned.

It was the only item in the room that had not been returned to its proper cupboard.

Her eyes settled on a vase of lilies on the counter, whose white petals were just beginning to unfurl.

What was it about the miracle of love that Hafez has written?

> *When destitute and in need, let your love and passion*
> *breed,*
> *Life's alchemy, essence and seed, unimagined wealth*
> *shall create.*

She thought of all the times in her life she had heard these words.

Closing the box of henna powder, Zadi returned it to the glass-fronted cupboard. Then she went back to her apartment.

Standing in the middle of the room, a person could hardly hear a sound, not from the corridor outside her door, let alone from the traffic of the avenue five flights below.

Zadi sank into one of the upholstered chairs closest to the door and brought her hands to her face. Running her fingers through her dark hair, she took in another deep breath.

The scent of henna had lingered, its acrid, woodsy aroma permeating the air. It suddenly hit her, heady and intoxicating.

That day by the Caspian Sea, during the solar eclipse, their high school teacher telling them the end of the world was nigh.

That poetry was their only answer.

She and her school friends had giggled then, impersonating their wacky teacher on the bus ride home, quoting him as much as they did the Hafez poem.

They had gotten in a lot of trouble for that, each of them sent home for a week with a letter of warning, but it had been worth it just to shout those lines, saying them the way they wanted to without a thought of the consequences. Irreverence was their ally.

Then there was the morning of her tenth birthday, when her grandmother had given her a singular pearl, the start of a necklace, she said, one that would be completed by the time Zadi began university. The opening of the oyster, the universe expanding, the molecules around your neck giving you voice to shout anything, Grandmother Shahrzad had said.

"But first there is love, the beginning of everything. Let that be your catalyst, your mother, your father."

When destitute and in need, let your love and passion
breed,
Life's alchemy, essence and seed, unimagined wealth
shall create.

Forgetting her usual deference for her sleeping neighbors, Zadi followed the dawning light that was streaming onto the landing.

The atrium with its windowpanes of juxtaposing glass sent rays straight into the building's lobby, splintering into a symphony of color—prismatic light that speckled every nook and cranny of the old, marble-floored entry.

Here on the fifth floor, it sent a diffused glow, soaking into all the walls and windows.

The doors that separated the various rooms and apartments on the fifth floor were made mostly of glass; only a panel of wood broke through the middle of each door, allowing for a handle and a keyhole. Were it not for the multicolored curtains that lined each apartment's facade, the activities of the various inhabitants would have been as visible as the sky shining through the roof. She was so startled to see the hole again—made by Maryam's little fist in the glass porthole, larger than she expected—that it took her a few moments to notice the Capitan.

"How is the little one?" he asked as she turned away from the door. He had not been able to sleep; there were dark rings under his already-sunken eyes, and his small patch of hair was standing at all angles on his head.

"She will be all right, Capitan," Zadi answered. She bit her lip, not wanting to tell him more than she had to.

She did not want to tell him what the doctors had said, how there could be a poison coursing through her baby's blood, taking over her little body.

Zadi looked up at the Capitan.

The old man did not look as though he could take any more bad news.

"I have to get back right away," Zadi said.

The Capitan nodded.

"Of course, of course. Give my love, give my blessings." He coughed.

"I will, Capitan. Get yourself to bed," Zadi said. She pulled the handle, looking at the gaping hole again. There was not much of the window left; the remaining shard had fallen during the course of the night, no doubt jostled by the many who had passed through the threshold.

"Zadi Khanoum?" The Capitan stepped forward. "There are different wells within us. Some fill with each good rain. Others are far, far too deep for that." He coughed again.

"Thank you, Capitan."

Zadi took the shards and walked to the kitchen, Hafez's lines ringing in her ears.

I know not who resides within my heart
though I am silent, he must shake and quake.
My heart is on fire, I can't sleep
where is the tavern I have hundred day headache.

Chapter Twelve

It is that old adage of consequence, thought the Capitan. The understanding of endings.

He leaned on his broom and looked up at the glass ceiling. The pigeons were doing their usual cooing on the ledge outside. The afternoon sky was hazy, as it had been all week. A chilled autumn breeze blew.

The Capitan knew this even without having felt it, for he rarely left the apartment building. But the awareness of the change was there, and it led him to confusion. Try as he might, he could not get used to the different sequence of seasons, the topsy-turvy exchange of winter for summer in this Southern Hemisphere.

He noticed a flock of traveling birds flying over the skylight, migrating to a warmer place, somewhere across the ocean.

Travel again? he thought. *Return to where I came from? No way. Enough.*

His mind had long ago come to terms with the idea. *Here is the end for me,* thought the Capitan, although deep inside, he wished to go back to Tabriz, to his birthplace, to meet old friends. But where were they? He was not sure whether any of his friends were still in Tabriz.

Strange how the soul yearns for what it knows, to return to its source, like the reed in Rumi's poem.

> *Listen to the story told by the reed,*
> *complaining of being separated.*
> *Since I was cut from the reed bed,*
> *through me, everyone has cried.*
> *I have a burning desire to tell,*
> *the story of my painful yearning.*
> *Anyone pulled from his base*
> *longs to go back to re-join again.*

The Capitan sighed. It was as much the truth as anything he had ever heard or read. And he had heard and read a great deal in his fifty years. It was one of those surprises of old age. How the words one has read nearly come to match the experiences of one's life.

Not exactly—but nearly.

The Capitan placed the broom back in its corner behind the kitchen door and returned to his apartment. There were still pieces of glass tucked into the grooves of the mosaic floor.

With his friends, the Capitan had watched as soldiers had taken captive their prime minister, Mossadegh, the one man who could have saved the country from that strange corruption, oil, and the greed that for the sake of vanities, had tied them to foreign places.

And he and his friends had gone to the capital, Tehrán, to do something about it.

All of them packed in that Vatan bus, taking to the raggedy roads that led through the ridges of the Sahand.

Those mountains, the valleys cleansed by the spring snows, did not prepare them for what they saw. The bloodshed was already in progress when they arrived at the university square.

Everyone had heard about or experienced what the supporters of the Shah had done. They could not believe what the Shah's propaganda was promoting through the radio and newspaper. The people heard the false rhetoric that the Shah had come to save the country. They heard it said so many times—the untruths were repeated so often—that they came to trust even the echoes of what they were told. And so it was during those days before their dear prime minister was taken from his home.

The Capitan and his friends believed in their prime minister's words, in his vision for the country. They saw what he wanted to do. They all wanted a part in this transference of power. So many were already turning away from what the Shah had been doing, rejecting his unquenchable thirst and the stupidity of his lot. People understood what they could become, what they really were without that greed pushing them along. And they saw all their hopes perish that day in Tehran.

Such a day it was, too. Clear skies; the vendors on the streets with their chilled rose-flavored drinks. And the group of them, students mostly, waiting for destiny.

There is nothing left of me.

Months had passed since he had arrived at Evin Jail. The friends with whom he had attended the protest were nowhere to be seen, not in any of the adjoining cells.

Why the Shah's police had not come looking for him sooner was a mystery. But they worked in ways no one really understood. Ways that made fear the permanent way.

He had been lying on a mat, staring at the brick walls of his cell. He had been listening to the various sounds, the cries and the prayers. He had been thinking that surely those bricks must be haunted, for all the misery they had seen.

And then he noticed that a single brick was slightly protruding from the wall in the darkness. He pulled the brick out and saw that a book had been stuffed into the hole behind the brick.

Someone had put a book of Hafez's poetry in the wall.

It fell open to a page:

> *Openly I admit and happy to say*
> *enslaved to your love, and I am free.*
> *I am a bird of paradise, have no longing*
> *in this trap of life and worthy tragedy.*

And so it was understood: the Capitan, from the alleys and soft steppes of Tabriz—he must take action. "We must seek our freedom in this place," he told his cell mates the following week. "We must make this happen." And so they formed a poetry circle.

Every week they would gather on their mats and read from the book. But not only from the book—they also read from the memory of their memories, which, until then, appeared to have disappeared. So it is with anything that is not always seen, and so it was with words.

Such beautiful and profoundly meaningful poetry, the Capitan thought, as he entered his hushed apartment. He sat on his carpet, crossing his thin legs. The poetry of Ferdowsi's *Shahnameh* and the great *Divan of Hafez*. To be told how the soul came into being. How it could flourish. Flourish when all was pushing for death, for destruction. To have heard it as a song from one heart to another.

What it meant to sing out those ghazals, to know that at the end of them came a repetition of a different kind, a push for something right. To understand and absorb the beauty of universal harmony.

We were all young, wanting, thought the Capitan. Knowing that to want is the right way of being. The way of life. And that the way to carry this thread inside was to seek it out. What better way than to immerse oneself in the rich words of Attar, Rumi, Hafez, and Nizami?

It was Nizami who understood the burning desire of the lover, his passion, his sacrifice, the inward fire of love and its outward manifestations.

The Capitan and his brothers talked of their beautiful beloved girls. Those girls they left behind in their past lives. For every one of them had a beloved one to think of, and to talk about.

"Oh, God was a man! God was a poet to have brought us those tears of understanding. Oh, to love as a young man, to want desire, to desire want!"

And so they spent their nights, free as ever, as they waited for their treason trials.

He had been in prison for ten years by then; going by the solipsistic nature of the Iranian penal system, vague and cruel, he looked to be there for infinity. The whole country was under military lockdown it seemed; the Shah's not-so-secret police, Savak, roaming the streets of all cities, looking for anyone with the slightest hint of rebellion.

News such as this would reach him and his fellow prisoners through Chinese whispers, in a roundabout way, through people who knew people or, like the Capitan, the right guards, the right words of poetry.

He had recited his way to knowledge, thought the Capitan, to knowing.

Zadi sat behind the counter, watching Haji Khanoum and Parastoo tend to their clients. It had been difficult for her to do much work the past few days; every attempt to rouse energy had failed. She was finding it difficult to accept the concerns of everyone who stepped into the salon and to hear them asking what had happened to Maryam.

She had spent most of her days and nights at the hospital, until Maryam's release yesterday. Sitting sentry the whole day, a chair propped next to Maryam's bed, she had watched her little one as Maryam slept; the girl's round face was tinged green, her hair plastered to her head.

A thick bandage wound around her tiny wrist.

The septicemia, which had been nearing, had decided at a crucial moment to take itself somewhere else, to wherever poisons went, mercifully leaving her baby's body.

Maryam's wrist had been severely cut, and there was an artery that had needed mending.

She would have a scar from the stitching, Sheema told her, but that would be the extent of the damage. The Capitan's daughter, along with the rest of the students at the hospital, had mended her.

A lie, Zadi thought.

No machine in the world could show what she knew: something had been broken beyond repair.

Nodding at the sympathies offered her way, Zadi left the salon and stepped out into the corridor. She could see Maryam in Haji Khanoum's apartment. She was lying on the daybed, listlessly thumbing through a book of fairy tales. She had not spoken since they had brought her back from the hospital. Refusing to answer any questions, she acknowledged Zadi only with the flicker of her eyes. Eyes that were filled with blame and anger. Another side effect, which Sheema had assured her would be remedied with time.

Zadi looked up at the atrium. A trio of birds was perched on one of the ledges that jutted out at its base. She could hear the voices chattering inside her salon.

.   .   .

Zadi cleaned up and laid out their beds for the evening. The two mats rolled out next to each other, near the bookcase with all its beautiful volumes. She slept deeply and calmly beside Maryam all night. She had not slept like that for so long—not since her days at the hammam. Growing up in Grandmother Shahrzad's house, she had a room for herself, a bed and mattress as she had had at home with her parents, but somehow she did not miss these luxuries when she was at the hammam.

Whether they were luxuries or not was a matter of contention. Zadi looked at her daughter. Maryam had fallen into a tenuous sleep. She had come back from the bathroom with Haji Khanoum, her face covered in rose cream, her little wrist washed and bandaged again.

"Did I pass on some strain of martyrdom to her?" Zadi had asked Haji Khanoum earlier that evening. "Did I give her a weakness without knowing?"

"Not weakness, joonam, *azizam*," Haji Khanoum replied, shaking her head. "Strength. Truth."

Zadi was not so sure. Something had made her say those words to her daughter. Something she had not thought existed inside. How could she have taunted her like that? What was within her that made her so weak?

It was against life to have acted in such a manner toward Maryam.

Homa Sookoot stared out from behind the stall table. The market was filled with vendors setting up for the day's sale. There were stalls for vegetables and woven goods. Nothing like the bazaars she had known, but she was glad for that. Everyone knew you in a bazaar. Here, people just thought them to be two more immigrants looking to eke out a living.

The paintings were marvelous. Even Homa was surprised by how they had turned out. Neither she nor Reza had ever trained in the art of painting, let alone in the intricate style of the Persian miniature; of course paintings such as this were everywhere in Iran, but until they had come here it had never occurred to her to create them herself.

Homa looked at the crowd milling through the market.

The plaza was as always lined with people, mostly women in white headscarves carrying placards. Something always stirred in her when she saw them. They derived, it seemed, from the same strain, from the impulse that had been the catalyst for her joining the Tudeh party while she was still at the University of Tehran.

It had been her duty, as it had been Reza's as well. They were following the line given to them by their parents.

I know what it means to follow your duty, thought Homa, *and what price you have to pay for following a line and a purpose.*

She had learned very early, as young as two, about duty, the duty to entertain her brother, and the duty of being submissive. That was when her older brother Pedram used to play his pillow game with her. One might say that there is very little, for an adult, to recollect of her life experiences at the age of two. But the daily torture Pedram liked to inflict on her was something Homa could remember with clarity.

It would happen when their mother was out of the room. That was when Pedram would take a pillow and come around to where she lay on the divan.

He would take the pillow and press it deep into her face. She remembers the loss of air and how everything went black around her for those few moments before he would laugh, lift the pillow, and walk away. Even back then she knew that if she was not careful, if she let on that she really didn't want to play, Pedram would keep on pressing that pillow over her mouth until she could no longer take another breath.

The pillow game eventually stopped when Pedram grew older and lost interest. He preferred to shoot at sparrows in the garden with his friends rather than bother with his little sister. But for her, the notion of duty stayed.

Chapter Thirteen

The poetry meetings resumed, even if Homa did not feel she could.

Tonight, they started with Rumi. Although the Capitan was bursting to open with Hafez, he had thought it best saved for later, as the evening progressed. *A fani, heech, nothing, as I am, should always give way,* he thought to himself.

After Haji Khanoum had finished the Zekr, Houshang started with a poem from Rumi:

> *To test her lover, she asked him,*
> *do you love more yourself or me?*
> *He replied, I am so vanished in you,*
> *that I became totally filled with you.*
> *Nothing left of me but a name,*
> *nothing exists in me but you.*
> *When a stone becomes ruby,*
> *it becomes full of sunlight.*
> *If that ruby loves itself,*
> *it means it loves the sun.*

If it loves the sun,
it means it loves itself.

Houshang paused and looked around. He seemed to be waiting for some words of admiration—or perhaps he was trying to express his own feelings.

"I think you have missed a bit," said Zadi. "Let me try." She began to recite, from memory:

To test her lover, she asked him,
do you love me or yourself more?
He replied, I am so vanished in you,
that I became totally filled by you.
Nothing left of me but a name;
nothing exists in me but you.
When a stone becomes a ruby,
it becomes full of sunlight.
If that ruby loves itself,
it means it loves the sun.
If it loves the sun,
it means it loves itself.

The Capitan opened his eyes. "We are going into the abyss now . . . we are getting it." He looked around. "And that is how Hallaj said, I am God and told the truth."

"Yes, but did he really?"

Haji Khanoum reached for a pistachio cookie. "Did he really speak the truth or was that just his animal desire, his nafs, speaking?"

"Ah, Haji Khanoum. But they are the same. They are all the same . . . the sunshine and the ruby. The earthly, the profane."

"Lover and the beloved awake. They had just made love. He had that on the brain."

"Yes, but . . ."

And so they continued into the night, turning over poetry and its meanings.

The culture of poetry and poetry reading has been cultivated by Iranians since antiquity. Poetry seems to be in their blood, in their genes. Avesta, the holy book of Zoroastrians, was written in verse. Every family has at least one book of poetry in the house, and that is *Divan of Hafez*, the works of Hafez, many written in beautiful Persian calligraphy and decorated with miniature paintings. The second most widely read book of poetry must be *Golestan* by Saadi, followed by the *Rubaiyat* of Khayyam, *The Masnavi* and *Kolliyat Shams* by Rumi, and *Shahnameh* by Ferdowsi. Of course, there are many famous contemporary Iranian poets; among them, Forugh Farrokhzad is the most respected and beloved of the women poets.

Iranian poets have been highly respected for their role in keeping their culture and language alive, despite many destructive foreign invasions. The literary masterpiece of Ferdowsi, *Shahnameh*, the Book of Kings, written in the tenth century, helped the Iranian language, culture, and ancient history to survive the Arab invasion. Iranians grow up reciting, memorizing, interpreting, discussing, and arguing relentlessly about the meaning of poems from their early school years, if not earlier. The beauty of these poems resides in their ambiguities. They require interpretation and discussion, and above all enjoyment. Iranian poetry surpasses any differences of culture, religion, and politics; it acts as an agent of unity for all Iranians.

. . .

Ah, to me, the real thing is, why is she asking him such a question? What kind of love does she have for him? Choosing between herself and him? the Capitan wondered.

Houshang Bahmanian took the book from the Capitan.

"Please wait," he said. "There is more to Rumi's poem:

> *To test her lover, she asked him,*
> *in the early morning hour,*
> *Sincerely, tell me the whole truth,*
> *do you love me more or yourself?*
> *He replied, I am so vanished in you,*
> *that I became totally filled with you.*
> *Nothing left of me but a name;*
> *nothing exists in me but you.*
> *When a stone becomes a ruby,*
> *it becomes full of sunlight.*
> *If that ruby loves itself,*
> *it means it loves the sun.*
> *If it loves the sun,*
> *it means it loves itself.*
> *Try hard to become less stone,*
> *so that your stone shines like a ruby.*
> *Become completely listening ears,*
> *so that you can make earrings from your ruby.*
> *Dig your well deep as a well-digger,*
> *so you reach your water within.*

"What kind of question is do you love me more or yourself? How is one supposed to answer that?" Houshang asked when he had finished reciting.

"Just as he did," the Capitan replied, sipping his tea. "The ruby and the sunlight are one."

"Not good enough." Houshang looked around the circle for support.

Reza Sookoot replied, "You're missing the point."

"The point is that Rumi wrote that because he had found true love," Haji Khanoum said. "And it was given back to him. A heartbroken person would not have been so quick to jump to such an ideal. Such easy giving."

The Capitan looked shocked. "Haji Khanoum, I am surprised at you. Of everyone here, I thought you would understand the poem the most."

"Why?" Haji Khanoum smiled slyly. "Because I contact the divine every morning?"

"Precisely because of it."

"That doesn't mean I am not a woman, the profane!"

Houshang sprang to his feet. "Ah! There we are, we finally get to the truth. A woman for you."

The Capitan looked up at him. "Now, wait a minute, young man . . ."

"Maybe we should have a break?" Zadi interrupted.

Next to her father, Sheema Bahrami nodded. Zadi turned to the couple across from her. Homa and Reza Sookoot looked beaten. Their days in the market were long, and they spent most nights painting the miniatures they sold.

Sheema looked tired, too. She had been working nearly nonstop the past week, checking on Maryam whenever she had a break from her studies, making sure to round up as much medicine from the hospital repository as she could. "A break would be good . . ."

They all shuffled out into the moonlit corridor.

The Capitan stared at the others, a look of sadness in his eyes. "I suppose . . . ," he said, sighing. "But—"

"Thank you, Capitan," Zadi said, feeling sorry to have to disappoint him.

Zadi remained at the salon door for a few moments. Haji Khanoum had taken Maryam to the kitchenette. Zadi looked to the other end of the corridor. She could see the Capitan and his daughter in their apartment; they had not drawn their curtains. The Capitan was staring at the floor, and his daughter disappeared to her side of the small room.

What was life like for them, Zadi wondered. Sheema was dutiful, but she did not seem to spend much time with her father. There seemed to be a chasm between them.

There was something about their daily exchanges that was painful to watch, thought Zadi, but she could not put her finger on it.

Zadi drew the curtains across the glass. She had once asked the landlord why the walls on the fifth floor were made of glass.

"The fifth floor," Niendo told her, "was an attic, where the owners before the current ones once kept doves. The patriarch of the family had a penchant for the winged creatures, thinking they contained the secrets of the magi and a bit of El Dorado's to top it off. A bit of a loony. After losing the building in a poker game, Señor had locked himself away with the doves and refused to come down until he was well and truly gone.

"Sorry! You asked, eh?" Niendo had added, chuckling as he hurried down the stairs.

She had heard stranger stories.

Haji Khanoum came back from the kitchenette with tea and biscuits. "Let's go back and read more poetry. I need some divine booster, maybe something from Attar?" Zadi called to everyone.

They sat in a circle, drinking tea. Haji Khanoum brought out the book *Divan Attar* and asked Houshang to recite a poem. Houshang knew just what to recite.

> *Butterflies gathered one night,*
> *to learn the truth about the candle light.*
> *And they decided one of them should go,*

to gather news of the beloved glow.
One butterfly from a distance he flew,
through the palace window he saw a candle glow,
and went no nearer: back again he flew,
to tell the others what he thought he knew.
The butterflies' mentor dismissed his claim,
saying that he knows nothing of the flame.
A butterfly more eager than the one before,
set out and passed beyond the palace door.
He flew through the air around the fire,
a trembling blur of timorous desire,
He flew back to say how far he had been,
and tell the story of what he had seen.
The mentor said: You have no more signs,
than the one before, of how the candle shines.

Haji Khanoum gave a low chuckle and nodded. Houshang cleared his throat and pushed his glasses back along the bridge of his nose.

Another butterfly embarked on a dancing flight,
sat on the blazing fire of candle light.
He immersed in the fire in his frenzied trance
both self and fire were mingled by his dance.
The flame engulfed him from head to toe,
in a translucent fiery red, his body glowed.
When the mentor saw the sudden blaze,
his form changed within the glowing rays.
He said: That butterfly knows truth we seek,
that hidden truth of which we cannot speak.

Houshang closed his eyes, his hands raised with his palms open.

"Yes, to acquire true knowledge, we need to learn how to become like the third butterfly: fearless," said the Capitan.

"Passionate," Zadi followed.

"Drunk," Haji Khanoum said quickly.

The lamps flickered and silence prevailed.

After everyone left, Zadi closed the door and sat down in an armchair to have a moment of silence with herself. Something new was on her mind, which had been demanding an answer. She remembered a few days before, when the landlord, Niendo, had knocked on the salon door. "Señora Zadi." Niendo had sniffed, scowling at the hole in the landing door. "I will need your services."

"Is this about the war?" Parastoo had asked, her voice trembling.

"What? Ah no! No!"

Haji Khanoum had walked in. "It's true. It's all over the television. Thatcher is coming." She turned to the scowling man. "Ah, Niendo, finally coming for that waxing?"

Niendo sniffed again. "You are lucky I have a soft heart. And don't even start with me on that broken door." He turned to Zadi, speaking in Spanish. "Señora, I need you to be here tomorrow night. You have a new tenant."

"You mean *you* have a new tenant," Zadi said.

"Whatever. Will you be here tomorrow night? You know I don't know your language. I will need you to translate."

"Where else would she be?" Haji Khanoum gave the landlord a look of disdain.

"Eh! Can't even have a conversation with you people! Don't get me started on that door!" Niendo waved his hand at the missing panel in the landing door and disappeared down the stairs.

Haji Khanoum patted for Narges Tapesh to resume her seat. "I had this dream once that Parastoo and I tied him down with some band thread and plucked his fat eyebrows really slowly. Do you think it means anything?"

Parastoo looked shocked. "I would never do that!"

"Sure you would," Haji Khanoum replied. "You were the one who suggested it."

Zadi had forgotten all about Niendo's request when he opened the landing door. "Señora Zadi."

Next to him stood a woman, dressed in dark clothes, wearing a headscarf, a rusari.

"Your new tenant."

He nodded at the woman, who hesitated, standing still by the door. Zadi stepped forward, holding out her hand. After a moment, the woman returned her handshake, raising her eyes to meet Zadi's gaze.

"Farzaneh Soltani," the woman whispered, her voice soft but steady.

"That's right. Soltan. These names. So hard to remember," the landlord said. "Soltan. Her name is Soltan."

"That is okay, Niendo. I got it. Thank you," said Zadi, smiling.

Odd as it sounds, I feel I know her already. But how is that possible? Her name, Farzaneh, sounds very familiar, but Soltani? Zadi thought.

There was something about her eyes; that look of struggle, which Zadi had seen looking back at her many times in the mirror, a kind of light that could dim as quickly as it could appear, without notice or warning. It comes from having witnessed too much sadness too quickly, that play of dark and light in the eyes, one she had seen in many other women.

Zadi wondered what had happened to the Farzaneh she had known, the Farzaneh of her memory. She had read and heard that that Farzaneh was in trouble because of her involvement in the Iranian women's movement.

Zadi felt confused. *I hope wherever she is, she has found some peace.*

That Farzaneh had been glorious and had been up to something that could change women's lives, Zadi thought. *But how could it be? If she is the same Farzaneh, why is she here? Why is her surname different? Soltani, instead of Farahanguiz?*

Chapter Fourteen

"Zadi-jan!" Houshang Bahmanian stood in the doorway.

Zadi quickly wiped away the tears that had gathered along her jawline and looked up.

Houshang cleared his throat. He ran his hands through his hair. "Now that war is breaking out . . ."

Zadi moved across the room and began to pull the curtain. "It's not a war."

"Can't you feel it, Zadi? It's happening everywhere. We can't run away from it. It still follows us." Houshang paused. He stepped forward. "Marry me!"

"What?"

"I love you. I have been in love with you since the first time we laid eyes on each other."

"Hello, gorgeous. Staying for tea?" Haji Khanoum walked in just then with a tray of sweets and a pot of tea from the kitchenette.

Houshang's face was pale and stricken. "No, thank you!" he nodded and disappeared back into the dark corridor.

Zadi, relieved, let out a breath.

"Maryam-joon is out. Out with that book she keeps under her pillow. She said the funniest thing about Thatcher—what's the matter, joonam? You look so pale."

Zadi wanted to keep Houshang's proposal as a secret, at least for now, so she cleverly diverted the subject.

"It's really happening then, Haji Khanoum? Another war?"

"Nothing to worry about, joon-e man. We'll be fine. The salon will be fine," Haji Khanoum sighed. "War. Always war."

"Why does it feel like I'm the one, Haji Khanoum, who's always fighting?"

"Come, sit with me here, little one," Haji Khanoum patted the carpet next to her. "Come, and tell me what is going on."

Zadi suddenly burst into tears.

"I don't know why I'm crying," she started, dabbing at her eyes again. "I'm not the kind of person who cries. Not ever. Even at my beloved grandmother's funeral, when the rest of the women in our family were shrouded in their black chadors, sitting in a circle around her withered, powdery body. Even then, I couldn't summon the weeping. It's just not the way I'm built, I suppose. There's a wall here inside my heart that stops the tears.

"We Iranians know about this wall. Like the walls around our houses and gardens, so high that not even the rooftops can be seen from the street. *Darun* and *birun*, the inside and the outside, are two different worlds, we are told. Keep them separate at all times. Do not forget.

"And if one day you dare to climb over that wall, to shout when you are to stay silent, to laugh when you should be crying, they lock the gate behind you.

"'You are *deevoon-e*, crazy, not safe to be around,' they will tell you.

"Me, I chose to laugh instead of cry. Instead of lowering my gaze, I looked up into a man's eyes, the blue eyes of a man who understood all about the weakness of walls.

"And for this they punished me in the worst possible way—they cut me off from her name . . ."

"My grandmother and I shared the same name. We were both called Shahrzad, after the famous storyteller of the *One Thousand and One Nights*.

"Like that black-eyed princess who saved an entire kingdom of women with her carpet stories, my grandmother was also of royal blood. She was born a Qajar. From a royal line, but not one immediate to the throne.

"Her summers as a child were spent on the Caspian Sea with the rest of the royal brood, and there was a yearly visit to the court during the coronation anniversary, but other than that she lived quite a normal life with her family in the town of Hamedan. She married her father's physician, a handsome young man who spoke five languages and loved to read out loud to her from books of Western philosophy, and they moved into a large, comfortable home across the street from her parents' house, a place with a large orchard of persimmon trees.

"She was not the most beautiful girl on her block, my grandmother Shahrzad, but she was by far the smartest and most practical, a quality most of the Qajars lacked.

"While her cousins were falling head over heels with opiated princes, losing themselves in excessive eating and palace intrigues, she was busy building her own little empire, a house filled with a fine collection of Safavian art, cozy library nooks, and the mess and laughter of her seven children. And when my parents died, it was she who took me in, brought me to live in her house.

"For this, and a thousand other reasons, I cherished the ground beneath her feet.

"Of my grandparents' seven children, only my two aunts and my father had remained in Iran.

"My uncles had all gone to schools in cold places like Switzerland and Scotland, met ginger-haired women with fire in their eyes, and married them.

"Had it happened to any other mother, it would have broken her heart, but my grandmother was philosophical about having sons who deserted her.

"'A daughter,' she would say, 'is a daughter for life. A son is a son only until he takes a wife,' a wise observation, but one that was hard to believe if you were to go by my aunts.

"Ameh Latifeh was the eldest. A moderate beauty when she was a teenager, she had accepted the hand of a much older man, one of Hamedan's wealthiest merchants. He was fat and pockmarked and smelled of fried fenugreek, which he consumed kilos of every day.

"His appetites also ran toward young boys, a cruel discovery for Ameh Latifeh. She became very bitter as a consequence.

"As for Ameh Tahereh, who possessed neither a memory of youthful good looks nor her eldest sister's cunning, she buried herself in Koran studies, and was known to use the belt on everyone from her children to the neighborhood dog as a form of personal penance.

"They were so envious of my grandmother's love for me. They hated how she allowed me freedoms they could never possess—they complained whenever I got a new outfit or whenever I went out with my friends to the movies.

"It was 1974, and the country was as free as it had ever been. Miniskirts and discotheques. Hands being held down every street, lips caressed. At eighteen I did not have a curfew, and was allowed trips to the local cinema and the Italian pizza café.

"It was at this cinema that I first fell in love with a man. Peter O'Toole. He was an English actor with blond hair and blue eyes.

"He played Lawrence in *Lawrence of Arabia*.

"Oh! My heart beat so fast the first time I saw him there on the big screen.

"I returned every day to watch the movie, until even the theater owner took pity on me and said I could go in for free.

"He told me to save the ticket money for makeup and pretty female things.

"I didn't like the way that theater owner looked at me.

"I didn't like how any Iranian boy or man looked at me, to be honest. My heart belonged to Peter O'Toole, that was it. I promised myself that the man I married would have to be Peter O'Toole, or someone who looked exactly like him.

"Someone with pale blue eyes and skin so white I could see his veins through it.

"Veins that would be pumping with love for me.

"And I found such a man, not long after turning eighteen.

"David—his name, as I learned later—wasn't an Englishman like Peter O'Toole, but the next best thing—an American. An American with blond hair and blue eyes.

"He was an architect, part of a team that was building a new bridge outside Hamedan. The bridge traveled over a brook that also passed by the back of my grandmother's home. It was bordered by walnut trees and fed by the Alvand Mountains.

"Oh, how I miss my Hamedan! I haven't been back since I was eighteen, you see, Haji Khanoum.

"I was rounding the street corner when I saw him. It was late September, but the summer heat was still beating down harshly in the mountain town. As early as eight in the morning, it was at ninety degrees. I don't know what I expected to see when I turned the corner, my pigtails flying behind me, but it was not a naked man, that was for sure.

"He was naked from the waist up, but that was more than I had ever seen of a man. You would not find an Iranian taking his shirt off in public, of course. But I supposed he had a good reason, working as he was with his team on that new bridge they were building.

"The bridge was at the edge of town, and David was part of the contracting team. Americans were all over Hamedan then. All over the country. Ever since World War II, they had been building in America, their offices and shopping centers, houses and swimming pools, gardens for all the neighbors to see. Unlike Iranians, who prefer high walls around their homes.

"'Americans do not have the problem of walls like we do,' Grandmother Shahrzad once said. 'Or maybe it is that their walls are invisible, which is more dangerous.'

"I did not remember my grandmother's words that day.

"What I did think was how beautiful the American looked, like a movie star. He was taking a break with his foreman, smoking a Camel cigarette.

"His hair was gold, pure gold, and his bare chest was dripping with sweat.

"I didn't cross over the bridge, of course. I wouldn't have, even if it were built. As much as Grandmother Shahrzad allowed me freedoms not given to many of my school friends, I would never be forgiven if I were seen with foreigners. My grandmother was brought up in a loyalist household after all. She hated how the Qajars, and then the Shah, had sold out to the English and the Americans. I would never have been forgiven if she heard that I had crossed that bridge.

"So I took the long path around, as I did every morning.

"I didn't even look back at the man with the golden head and bare chest, even though my heart was thumping so hard I could see it moving against my school uniform.

"All day long I daydreamed about the golden man. I saw him turned out in a white turban, just like Lawrence had been in the desert, as he swooped me up on his stallion and took me away. Oh! Why couldn't I have this man, I thought, instead of the dark, mustachioed boys around me, who all wanted to corner you in some alleyway and probe your virginity with ugly smiles on their faces? I never wanted that for myself.

"'Be careful what you wish for,' the genie told Aladdin, and I should have listened as well.

"I should have thought twice about my desire before turning to it. I should have kept my fantasy locked away behind the gate. Instead, I walked up to the man with the golden hair the following week, and took one of those Camel cigarettes."

"I was making my way to school when I saw him again. He was helping his men crank start one of the cranes near the bridge. My thoughts were consumed by the color of his hair, the white and pink of his skin. Oh, he was so handsome!

"He was my destiny, I decided, and I was going to him. So I took my courage and put it all into my stomach, and let it lead me to the brook and that Lawrence of Arabia. And when he gave me a cigarette and lit it for me, I did not dare say no. I didn't want him to think me a simple country girl.

"He did not ask me if I wanted one, he just pointed the packet my way. 'I'm studying law next year,' I said, in my best American accent, as I took one of the cigarettes. I could speak fluent English from the age of six, as is normal for all schoolchildren, of course. We are all taught such fundamentals, at least we were when I was a girl. His men must have thought we were crazy, a schoolgirl from Hamedan and an American man, smoking every Monday morning and talking of nonsense. We talked about the weather that first day, meaningless things.

"He was twenty-seven, he told me, from a small place in Iowa. Had I ever heard of it? 'Nothing like the skies over Iowa,' he said.

"'Endless. That's what they are. Go on forever, beating out the Rockies, the fields, everything. That's what America's like, Zadi. Nothing to stop you from getting what you want there. Not like what you have here.'

"He threw his finished cigarette into the water and shook his head. 'Those mountains over there, the ones you love, they stop the sky, see. They're what we call an eyesore in architecture. They don't meld. They're there to keep things out. Keep things in,' he turned his blue eyes on me. 'That's not what you're like at all, Zadi. You need to know there's nothing anchoring you down. You need to be free.'

"And so it became our morning ritual, meeting around the bend near the river, talking of silly things. Wondrous things.

"The weather that first day, but then politics and freedom.

"I told him of my ambitions, of wanting to study prelaw at Tehran University, with plans to take it all the way to a degree. Six years to pass the bar.

"He quoted a poem he had recently read in a magazine.

> *Rise up sister and uproot the roots of oppression.*
> *Give comfort to your bleeding heart.*
> *For the sake of your freedom,*
> *strive to change the law. Rise up!*

"It was out of context—the lines meant something else entirely—but it did not matter. He was on my side. He wanted me to rise.

"I was in love with him.

"I had not done anything with him, of course, nothing to be ashamed of, but I still did not tell anyone of those morning meetings. The conversations. I knew I wanted to be with him, go where he would go, but the how and when—it all seemed insurmountable. Everywhere I turned there was a problem. And then there was my beloved grandmother, who had taken me in at the age of seven, giving me all the freedom a girl could get her hands on in Iran. How could I throw that back in her face?

"But there had to be a way.

Our longing is the way.

"The way came suddenly that spring."

"The day I lost my name. It was 20 March 1977. The day before *Nourooz*, the New Year celebration. What a glorious day it started out as, what joy I felt that morning.

"How precisely pungent everything smelled, how filled with life and springtime promise.

"All over Hamedan, New Year preparations were in full swing. Carpets were hung on walls and beaten until the dust left and the threads were bright. The air smelled of fresh *barbari* bread and saffron cookies.

"In the spring season, everything in life is renewed. People who can afford to, buy new clothes, carpets, furniture, decoration, and so on. If not, they wash, repaint, and clean everything.

"From gardens and courtyards, daffodils and tulips were being plucked for indoor vases and the smoke of woodsy incense filled the thresholds of houses, barring entry to any lingering winter spirits.

"There was much laughter to be had during this time as well, especially among the neighborhood children, who were eagerly awaiting the arrival of the Haji Firooz, the New Year's clown who smacked his tambourine and danced at each doorway for a little donation.

"I had always had a certain fear of the Haji Firooz clown as a child.

"There was something sinister about his black face paint and red costume, something of the devil in it, I thought. Whenever I heard the jingle jangle of his tambourine coming up the block, I would run inside the green metal gate of my grandmother's home and hide behind the biggest persimmon tree. I would wait under this veil of fruit until my heart stopped tearing at my chest and the jingle jangle was on its way to another neighborhood street. My grandmother Shahrzad knew of my fear and never pushed me to play with the Haji Firooz like the other children did. She never made any of her children do anything that frightened them. One of her many fine qualities.

"On that day, the one before the New Year, preparations were going on everywhere, none more so than within the walls of Persimmon Palace. Food was bubbling away on stovetops, and all the corners of the house were wiped down with rosewater rinse, filling it with the most awakening of smells, that of luscious roses.

"Like the furniture, all the carpets in the house had been washed and made ready weeks ahead of the New Year. But the servants who tended such matters had somehow overlooked the long runner in the hallway. The runner came from Tabriz, that city of handwoven carpets, and had a design of kissing turtle doves in its center.

"Instead of letting a servant roll it out in the courtyard and pour detergent on it, my grandmother insisted on washing the last carpet herself.

"It gave her pleasure to push her toes through the silk thread. 'To feel the pattern beneath the pattern,' she would say.

"And so no one thought it strange when she took the runner from one of the servant's hands and started to glide across its foamy surface in the courtyard.

"No one except for my aunts, of course. They were mortified.

"Ameh Latifeh remained tight-lipped, but Ameh Tahereh voiced her objections when she saw her mother doing a menial chore.

"'Thank God there are walls around this place,' she said. 'I would die if the neighbors saw this.'

"'Isn't it enough that God sees it? Isn't it enough that she is completely messing with the order of things, as she always does? Honestly, I think we need to have a serious talk with her. She needs to go to the Caspian for a while and get some salt air to clean that soft mind of hers.'

"Ameh Latifeh huffed up the stone steps that led from the courtyard into the house, throwing me a dirty look as she went. I was sitting in a wicker seat, popping beans out of their string beds. The beans would go into dill and butter rice, one of my grandmother's favorite meals for the New Year. That whole night, servants and household alike would be staying up cooking, preparing the endless dishes that would be served to the family and guests who would stream into the house at all hours during the thirteen celebration days. Cooking was one chore that was exalted, even by my aunts.

"I remember I was popping a bean out of its house, smiling at the sound it made when it jumped out into the sunlight, when Grandmother Shahrzad's head hit the ground. It took me a moment to realize that a bean did not make that kind of thud when released from its pod. I let go of the bowl of beans, spilling them as I ran to my grandmother's side.

"The foam on the carpet rose around her body, but it had not protected her skull. The doctor said it didn't matter, that she was already dead from an aneurysm, even before her head hit the limestone tiles of the courtyard.

"She had died by the time her feet were up in the air, her eyes looking to the heavens above.

"She was gone. And so was I," Zadi recalled.

"I ran. I ran from that house, from the funeral crowd that had come to eat not the food of new beginnings, but the morsels of memory.

"As my aunts covered themselves with their mourning chadors and began to wail the cry of the misbegotten—'To whom are you leaving us? To whom are you leaving us?'—pounding and tearing at the folds of their veils and chests like crazed animals, I wrapped my hair in my grandmother's favorite headscarf and tore out of home.

"My mind was blank, my heart untouchable. I could hardly see my way down our streets, past the midnight celebrations that were already beginning in every household but ours.

"I could still hear the mourning, wailing voices of my aunts as I ran.

"'To whom are you leaving us? To whom are you leaving us?'

"They seemed not to notice anything but their own grief, their own selfishness over the will of what was above.

"Didn't they know their faith well enough? Were they not aware that their wails were only paining Grandmother Shahrzad's rising soul as she took her leave?

"Where was their humility in the face of God?"

"I kept repeating these questions in my head as my own form of mourning, for I knew that I could not ask the same questions of my grandmother.

"I could not ask her to stay.

"She had been ready to go, there on the carpet, had chosen that moment when her toes were poised on the wings of doves to leave the earth.

"Or it was chosen for her.

"It was her time, simple as that.

"Still, I could not stop my running. I ran and ran until I came to the town square. The square in Hamedan is not really a square but a circle, the middle heart of a bigger circle. From this middle, there are six avenues like the spokes of a wheel, going off in every direction, and they are connected by a round road. Go south, and you get to the grave of Avicenna. That is the great medicine man. He is the one who first drew the essence from those rose petals, who discovered how to do it. But even he could not bring my grandmother Shahrzad back to life. To go northwest would take you to another tomb, that of Baba Taher. He wrote poems for the common man. For his baring of the purest of words, he came to be called 'The Naked,' but all of this is not as important as the fact that I was still standing in this circle square, unable to decide on anything, unable to see straight. It was then that I realized I had not been crying as I thought. That the grief inside me had turned into its own skin, had buried itself so deep the moment I heard my grandmother's head hit the ground.

"It was not going to come out even if I got down on my knees and dug with both hands. There is a poem by Rumi, a saying that is precious to many Iranians. You would know it, it goes

The seeker shall find
If you dig your well deep
You will reach the water within.

"But my well was already too deep. It seemed too dark for any tears.

"I stood in the middle of all those roads for I don't know how long. But it must have been some time before I realized that I was alone. That the sky was a strange burgundy color and that the spring day had become a cold wintry night.

"I was freezing and without a coat. I had run out of the house with only what I had on, bell-bottom jeans and a light sweater, and that black-and-white headscarf that smelled of my grandmother."

· · ·

"'Hey there. Aren't you supposed to be tucked into bed by now?'

"He was sitting on one of the stone benches to my left. A cigarette dangling from his mouth and a coat of long leather around his tall frame. My American.

"I thought I couldn't hold any more shock inside my body, but I was wrong. When I saw David, all I could do was fall, right there in the middle of the square, right there on the cold tiles.

"'Hey, hey.' David was at my side and lifting me up. He scooped me and put me on the bench and began to undo my headscarf. I don't think I was breathing, or I must not have been making any noise, because even an American knew not to touch a woman in public like he was doing. No man other than a husband was allowed to remove a woman's scarf, and I would have told David this if I could have found my tongue.

"I didn't find it, but he found mine. Because the next thing I knew, his mouth was joining with me.

"I could smell cigarettes and mint and all I could think of doing was fainting. It was the first kiss I had ever had, so what did I know about such things?

"How did I know that it wasn't a real kiss? That he was trying to breathe life into my body because he thought I was dying?

"I thought it was because he loved me.

"Why else did he keep whispering, 'Don't go on me now. Don't go anywhere, Zadi.'

"He was the first one to call me Zadi. I remember trying to tell him the story behind my name, about the princess Shahrzad and how she had come to be so amazing to all Persian women, but all he could do was shake his head again. 'It's too complicated, too long. I know you. You're simpler than that. You're a Zadi. That's what you are. That's what they'll call you back home. Zadi. It's friendlier, you know?'

"And I did. I did think it was easier, friendlier. Of course I was a Zadi.

"I had a quickening to my step after that renaming. I was no longer bound to the ground and walls of my grandmother's house. Suddenly Hamedan was too small for me, its streets and old-fashioned trolleys embarrassing to my eyes. I began to dread going to the bazaar, having to deal with the many intricacies of daily life. The kinds of things Iranians thrive on, live on.

"The way we have to *taarof* everything, that false humility, pretending we don't want something two times before accepting it the third. It isn't enough that we do it over a sofreh of food and at the bazaar. We even do it at weddings. The bride, pretending to be innocent, pretending not to want love. Just a farce. That wasn't real. David was right. We complicated things too much in Iran. If you want something, go after it. Shout it over the rooftops. Tell the world. What are all these false ways for?

"I had been thinking all of these thoughts those weeks, that whole autumn. So much was going on in my mind, round and round, making me dizzy with possibilities.

"The possibilities of a future that had suddenly begun to clear its way for me.

"A future beyond the peaks of the Alvand Mountains.

"I was in love with him. In such deep want of his arms, of his blue eyes, that I even began to neglect my studies. I had wanted to study law since I was a girl of fourteen. I wanted to follow in the footsteps of all the women who were rising up, answering the call to create a better country. For women to understand. Women know that no society can survive if their mothers and sisters are kept with rags in their mouths. With no words to say and no way of saying them. To cut the womb out of this world, to keep it behind high walls, is to go against everything natural. It is against God and against life. To be silent is to die. But to speak at the wrong time is death, too. You must choose when to keep the words inside. But sometimes, you can't help it. Sometimes, the words are already out of your mouth before you have thought them.

"And sometimes others choose those words for you, sealing your destiny.

"That is exactly what happened to me.

"I remember that first kiss from my American, there on that stone bench in that circle square in Hamedan.

"I remember how I raised my weakened arms and pulled on his neck, holding on.

"I remember him lifting me up, carrying me in his arms across that empty square, to his car parked in a side street.

"I remember not seeing anything of the streets as they flew past me, rattling my atoms, sending me into another space and time.

"Somewhere that car stopped. Somewhere time stopped as David and I kissed in that car.

"My essence was seeping out of me.

"I was rising out of my depths, unanchored. I heard the jingle jangle. I heard it for what seemed hours. I thought it was my heart, rippling like the ocean it was there in my chest, under where David lay. And when it stopped outside the car window, I did not think it strange, feeling that it was finally calm and no longer needed to keep beating against the rest of me.

"I thought of all of this even as I looked up and saw, in the reflection of the opposite glass, the face of all black.

"That face paint and red hat. That tambourine raised to a sharp-toothed grin.

"I blinked, then looked over David's shoulder to the car window. There was no face looking back at me. I was only dreaming.

"But I was wrong. The devil was looking right into my soul. The Haji Firooz had finally caught up with me, and there was no way of hiding."

. . .

"The Haji Firooz, the New Year's clown, was a local musician, a man who played at various tea shops around Hamedan. Once a year he would dress up and play that tambourine. He knew who I was and he knew where I lived.

"There was no doubt that he would soon tell my aunts what he had seen in the backseat of the American architect's car.

"David and I spent the night at the apartment where he was staying. The night was filled with both the joy of being together and the fear of being killed the next day by either my relatives or an angry mob. It was common in Hamedan for fanatically religious people to take justice into their own hands, and to punish with death anyone identified as a slut, a whore, or an infidel. I did not know what David was thinking, but I knew that my life as I knew it had come to an end.

"When I woke up, it was late the next morning. David had packed and gone. No trace of him was evident. I went quickly downstairs to the reception desk. The clerk told me David had checked out earlier in the morning. I rushed to my grandmother's house. I was so naive about it all. I gave no thought to what was waiting for me. I just knew I was scared and angry.

"My lover had gone. The whole town knew about it, thanks to the Firooz. The men from one of the tea shops went looking for him, meaning to bring him to justice. When they found out he had already left town, they got even angrier.

"The men of our neighborhood were yelling for blood, they were so angry. Not that having sex with an Iranian girl was illegal or anything—there were plenty of American men getting themselves Persian brides back then—but it was still a point of pride. I was from a Qajar family, one of the oldest in town. Not to mention that my grandmother had died the previous morning, so it was a double insult.

"I could hear the wailing again even before I slipped inside those green gates, but what I wasn't prepared for was what I saw in the courtyard. There, in one corner of the walkway, was a large bonfire, burning bright. All the guests who'd been at the wake were gone, and there were my two aunts. In the courtyard, wailing. They were throwing things into the fire. For one moment, I thought it was the Wednesday Fire Festival, the one that you jump over on the Wednesday before New Year. My grandmother had jumped that fire only a few days ago, I remembered. She had held her skirt and leaped, chanting the good-luck wish, asking the flames to give her strength for another year. I had done the same, rolling up the cuffs of my bell-bottoms, closing my eyes so that I could show my faith in being guided to a safe and cool spot on the other side, without looking.

"But that fire in the courtyard was not one of good fortune. It was one of destruction. My aunts were burning everything I ever owned. Every last piece that was mine. In the morning I was also banished, told never to return to Hamedan. Never to use my grandmother's name, our family name, as my own. Those two women sent me packing with nothing, nothing but the little nut growing inside my belly. A baby."

Zadi looked up at Haji Khanoum. Her eyes had a pained, determined look to them.

"I would soon discover how much I was going to need that strength of fire. I was going to need plenty of it. A never-ending flame."

Chapter Fifteen

Fortunes are strange things, thought the Capitan.

He thought of a film he had seen about fortunes on Haji Khanoum's television set. He would sometimes go over there after supper to enjoy cups of tea and *sohbat.* He had thought nothing improper about this, and neither should he, the fine lady assured him, when he raised the issue. How he would have liked to tell her more, how ridiculously his heart beat for her, but he could never, never.

> *I have estimated the influence of Reason upon Love,*
> *and found that it is like that of a raindrop upon the*
> *ocean.*

Tonight, there was a film on television, *Papillon,* starring Steve McQueen. He was named Papillon because of the butterfly tattooed on his chest. The Capitan had been invited by Haji Khanoum to watch the movie with her. For some reason, the movie made him think of the time when his daughter had caught a butterfly. The story her mother wrote to him because he was not there to witness it himself. Little Sheema had gone on an outing to those steppes above Tabriz and found herself a winged partner. A butterfly the size of her palm. With powdery wings that would blind a grown man for a week. Her mother had warned her not to touch the wings, but she touched them; she did. Going blind for three days for the love of such a beautiful thing.

The Capitan had found an admirable soul mate and an enthusiastic listener to whom he could tell his stories. The stories that had been kept within—a lifetime of precious treasures waiting to be presented to someone worthy of possessing and safeguarding them.

The secret that I never told and never will,
now, to my confidant mate, I'll tell.

"That film was interesting, but it was not like that for us at Evin," said the Capitan after the movie finished. "Unlike Steve McQueen, we did not even have the luxury of thinking of escape, let alone the opportunity to jump off a cliff, straight into a welcoming ocean."

Into a sacred existence that surpasses every existence.

"We were given one reprieve, and that was of prayer. This we were allowed in the mornings, though it was not a practice that was looked on as desirable. After all, it was the new age. The Shah, we heard—from other, newer prisoners—was putting rules in every corner of our world.

"My cell mates and I were reciting *Shahnameh* when a guard whispered to us of the Shah's return. The radio had broadcast the news to the whole country. His return, the Americans, President Eisenhower, the helicopters, and much more.

"Interestingly, I had chosen the story of metallurgy for that week's poetry meeting. The poem told the story of how that frenzied art was born, starting with the spark that was launched with the throwing of flint and the flame. The idea of alchemy in its purest form made me feel like we were free, and we could do anything we wanted.

"It was enough to make the four of us forget about things for a while, forget that there were things not right about the world outside, about our beloved country. And it made us remember other things. About the essence of what it meant to be an Iranian, a man. All we could do was try to remember, and help each other, by exchanging words back and forth. To remember, again and again, our past, our right to freedom, and to weave the carpet of our memories and stories.

"And so throughout our days in prison, we endured the worst kind of labor—that of doing nothing. We were given no duties in the prison and no information about the outside world. About what our fates would be.

"Would that we were able to recite poetry all the time, to have our meetings. But that was not possible. So we all sat.

"Sitting in the darkness.

"What madness is created in such moments."

The Capitan stopped, feeling sick in his stomach, like there was a heavy lump ready to burst out, crying. But how could he?

He was a man!

Haji Khanoum, realizing what was happening within the Capitan, said, "It is okay, it is good to let it out. I am here for you. Let's have a cup of tea and we will continue another day."

To prepare the henna, infuse tea leaves for five hours after it has boiled. Add clove oil and infuse for another three hours. This mixture should then be left overnight, before the henna can be added.

Zadi had done so the night before, boiling three batches in deep copper pots in the small kitchen in the back of the salon. She usually made only one batch for tattooing, but as the salon was hosting a bridal party over the next few days, she had decided to triple the amount for safety's sake. After cooling in a bucket of ice, the batches would be transferred onto plates wide enough for several brushes to dip at once.

The henna leaves were pale green in color. Before she had left that morning, Sheema Bahrami had stopped in with a bushel of them. A friend of hers at the university, she said, had access to a nursery.

"It's the acidity in the plant that makes it smell like the *Sahra*. I smelled it on my way to Mecca. Yes, I actually walked some of the way there," said Haji Khanoum.

"Why did you do it, Haji Khanoum? I always meant to ask. Why did you go to Mecca? You don't subscribe to any one religion. You're not exactly what I would call religious," Sheema said.

"When love sends you scattering along the face of this earth, you do what you can to find your spot on the ground. Even if it can't ever really be found."

It was a rainy day, and very quiet, only two clients in the early afternoon. The four of them got a chance to chat in peace. Zadi decided to teach Parastoo and Homa how to mix henna.

Following Zadi's instructions, Parastoo mixed the henna with the hot water. Unlike the henna used for hair dyeing, the henna paste for the bridal ritual is dark in color. Zadi instructed her while talking about her grandmother. Zadi could see her grandmother, mixing the henna, both for her hair and for her hands; she would do this herself even though she could afford to visit the beauty salon.

Later, at the hammam, Zadi learned a more precise way. She smelled the crushed leaves and was told about the Song of Solomon.

> *My beloved is unto me as a cluster of camphire,*
> *in the garden of En-gedi.*
> *Let us see if the henna has flowered,*
> *if the blossoms have opened,*
> *if the pomegranates are in bloom . . .*

"Homa! What is going on? You have been very quiet. You don't seem happy. I feel something is bothering you. It has to do with Reza, hasn't it?" asked Zadi.

"It is all men's fault," said Parastoo. Haji Khanoum interrupted. "Let her talk."

"I don't know what to say," said Homa.

Oh I know not who resides within my weary heart,
Though I am silent, she is shouting out loud.

"I married Reza a year after our meeting. We moved into a small house in the middle of town and began respectable jobs. Reza as a researcher in a university, and I in a shop that sold pottery and beautiful household things to rich housewives. We were not supposed to show any signs of belonging to the party. Officially we were no longer a living thing, but everyone knew that the Tudeh was still around and going strong. We had a hand in a lot of what was happening then in Iran, from the uprisings in oil fields to the university in Tehran. But the prize was going to come the following year. Reza and I were both called on to organize our division, to get our members bussed to the sites. This kind of thing was second nature to us. We never questioned our duty to our families and to the greater good. We understood that we were a collective of individuals, each of us with a responsibility. We were going to bring the country to a point where we no longer had to rely on one father to rule its destiny. That is the problem with our people. They never think they have the ability to move without looking to a greater baba, a monarch or king to tell them yes or no. What is it about so many of us that makes us so afraid to see the picture from another angle? To let go of the need to rely on someone who claims he knows more than all the others?

"Well, these were the ideas we were taught and brought up with, Reza and I. And we lived by them as well. And then the hostages were taken at the embassy.

"We watched our television. We saw the days unfold. The hostages were being brought out into the daylight of the American Embassy courtyard, for show. For the world was watching. Everyone was holding their breath to see what was going to happen. Whether the revolutionary students would kill any of the Americans.

"Whether President Jimmy Carter in Washington would bring down an army of helicopters to rain bullets on everyone.

"On the streets of Tehran, the madness was never-ending. The unraveling was horrific.

"Paykans and army jeeps driven by the rebels, flying down avenues that were deserted of pedestrians. Television crews filming it all so that we could see.

"Until that moment, the moment when the hostages were taken, I did not really consider leaving my country. I knew Reza had his ideas, his plans for the party, and so did I, but if I was going to be honest with myself, I had to admit that I never really believed they would come true. I know this now. But this was only a feeling, and a vague one, back then.

"We were watching television when the knock came.

"'Who is it?'

"'Open the door! Open the door, for God's sake! I'm about to die out here!'

"It was our landlady. Reza unbolted the door and let Fereshteh Emami in. She had a wild look in her eyes. She had her black rusari in her hand, instead of on her head, and was waving it frantically.

"'Lock the door! Lock the door!' she yelled, running right into the middle of our living room. 'God help us, they are everywhere!'

"'What's the matter, Fereshteh Khanoum? Are you in trouble?' I went up to her. I could see Reza already fuming. He never had much time for our landlady. He disliked her busybody ways, he said.

"'Trouble? Look at this here! This is trouble! This is the end of the world!' She pointed to the television screen. Machine-gun fire was erupting in the middle of a street. People were screaming. 'I have to get out of this city. Out of here!'

"Reza turned the television volume down, gritting his teeth. I turned back to Fereshteh Emami. 'But, Fereshteh Khanoum, you see yourself this is impossible. It's not safe for any of us to be out on the streets.'

"'No! You don't understand. They'll kill me if they find me. They'd kill me now if they knew where I was!' Fereshteh Emami sat down on our divan and broke into ragged tears. Her rusari was still in her hands. She used it to blow her nose.

"'Who will kill you?' I asked, sitting down next to her. Although we had been living below her for nearly a year, it was the first time we had ever had her inside our home.

"Fereshteh Emami let out a sob. 'Those crazies! Those revolutionary students across the street said not only are they taking over the American Embassy, but they are going around all the houses, looking for all the Baha'i. The Mullahs themselves said they can kill any Baha'i they find. That it won't be against the law in the new regime! Ah!' She started crying louder than ever.

"Just then, a woman in a rusari and chador appeared on the television. She was outside the American Embassy, surrounded by students from the university and other men. Reza turned up the volume on the television.

"The huge crowd of demonstrators was chanting, 'Death to America!'

"'Ah!' Fereshteh Emami stood up, screaming. Her hands were in the air. 'I've got to get out of here! They are going to kill me!'

"And just like that, she unbolted our door and ran out. And she was right.

"When the hostages were taken, I knew we were going to have to leave Iran.

"But to do what we did. To take what we took in order to fulfill that destiny. That, I could never have imagined. To take the very essence of someone's life—that was something I had never planned."

"Fereshteh Emami owned the small house, part of which we rented in the southern suburbs of Tehran. She was a widow and of Baha'i religion. I never really knew any Baha'i, not personally. Like those of the Jewish religion, who kept to their own quarter in town, Baha'i also stayed to their own kind. Being without any defined leaders, they had no places to worship besides their own homes, which was a good thing for them, really. Because the truth was that they were not liked by many in the country. They were even less popular than our own Tudeh, and we had long left God to the realm of the superstitious.

"Fereshteh Emami was a talker, that I really remember. She liked nothing better than to gossip about all the neighbors. She would sit on her balcony out the back, spying over the walls of the surrounding houses.

"She had bought a pair of binoculars at the bazaar and used them to her advantage, taking in the fights and love affairs of everyone around us.

"Reza and I had to keep our voices low in our downstairs apartment, because we were sure that she had some sort of device to pick up sounds tucked away inside our place downstairs as well.

"Our landlady had no idea we were communists. Had she known, she would probably have tried to convert us to her religion. We told her we were atheists. That was enough to frighten her into silence.

"Strange, how the very news she craved brought her to her end and brought us to what we thought was a beginning. Now I wonder whether it wasn't the other way around, whether our landlady found peace and we an eternity of pain.

"We decided to go back to Mashhad. We were to stay with Reza's mother and wait out what was happening. Then we would go to America, Reza said.

"We packed our bags, thinking we might take a train. Trains were still running across the country, but only just. As for airplanes—forget it. You had to be rich. One of the Shah's men had reportedly gotten one out during the madness.

"I thought of Fereshteh Emami, and how she had run out of our apartment, screaming. We had not heard from her since.

"'Do you think we should call on her, Reza?' I asked as we stepped out into the hallway that led from our apartment. As in the rest of the house, the floor was covered in little blue-and-white mosaic tiles. It was a cheaply built place, but even in the most humble of buildings you could find the work of artisans. That is our Iran, yes? Beauty, even in the midst of dilapidation and despair.

"Reza just looked at me as though I had gone soft in the head. He grabbed our suitcases and made his way to the front door. No taxi was going to pick us up, not when there was so much violence in and around our neighborhood. We were going to take our own Jeep to the railway station.

"'But she might want to know we are leaving. She might need something,' I said, my heart suddenly aching for Fereshteh Emami and how alone she was.

"Where would she go when the revolutionaries eventually came calling?

"'Maybe we could give her some advice.' I turned to the staircase leading up to our landlady's apartment.

"'Homa, get back here! You stupid girl!' Reza barked at me.

"But I was not listening.

"I quickly made my way up to the landing. Reza bounded after me, about to yell again, when he, too, understood what I had sensed.

"The door to Fereshteh Emami's apartment was ajar. Her body was in the middle of her living room. She was wearing her rusari, one hand across her chest, the other reaching out across the rug. Her eyes were closed. She was dead. Or at least that is what I thought.

"So did Reza. Because the next thing he did was charge through Fereshteh Emami's apartment, grabbing everything of value he could find.

"I stood with my mouth open, unable to say a word as he ransacked the place, finding money in sterling and tomans, even some American bills. He found jewels in boxes and drawers. He took pearl necklaces and a pair of diamond earrings that would later buy our tickets to Turkey.

"He gathered everything together as I stood watching.

"He did not even stop to look at me, to ask what possibly could have happened to our landlady, how she had come to die there in the middle of her living room floor. He took and took, stuffing it all into our pockets and suitcases. It was madness. It was a hunger, a shameful one.

"Whoever had done harm to Fereshteh Emami had not wanted to rob her. To extinguish her had been enough, it seemed.

"I did not want to look at her. I tried not to as Reza pushed closed a final drawer, shaking his head. I was out the door and about to step down the stairs when I turned around. Reza was kneeling at our landlady's body. He was doing something to her.

"I rushed back in. 'What are you doing?' I whispered, aghast. There was Reza, his hand around Fereshteh Emami's finger, wrenching something free. It was a ruby ring.

"My husband got up, the red jewel pinched between his thumb and forefinger. 'It does nothing for her now, Homa. This is our ticket, our way.'

"I was speechless. I had nothing to say. And then I saw the worst of it. For Fereshteh Emami was not dead. She had still been breathing as Reza took that ring from her finger. And he had seen it as well.

"He had chosen our moment, that turn that decided everything.

"And I knew that we were going to have to pay for what Reza had just done. For the pillaging in which I had partaken."

Chapter Sixteen

They had already made the rounds of reciting when the shadow passed along the corridor.

"Well, look who it is," said Haji Khanoum. Quickly reaching the door, Zadi found the new tenant just in time as she was stepping onto the stairs.

"Khanoum Soltani."

The woman turned around. She was wearing the same rusari she had on the day she arrived.

Zadi took another step forward. "I was just thinking you might like to join us. We're having one of our poetry nights. We meet once a week."

"I was going for a walk." Farzaneh Soltani looked at the stairs.

"In this weather?"

Zadi looked up at the skylight, above which gray clouds were forming.

Farzaneh stared at her.

"Please, Khanoum Soltani." Zadi, gesturing with open arms, turned toward the apartment door.

Introductions were made, and a space was cleared on the rug next to Homa Sookoot, who, Zadi noticed, was biting her bottom lip. From excitement, probably. There was a marked change in the air suddenly, if she was not mistaken. Everyone seemed to be beaming and smiling. Even Houshang had perked up out of his scowling state and was looking at the new tenant with interest.

"Why don't we ask our new arrival what she would like to hear? Or recite. It's up to you, Khanoum Soltani." Haji Khanoum handed her a glass of tea. Farzaneh looked at the carpet. She looked up at Haji Khanoum.

"You want me to suggest?"

"That's how it works here. Whatever comes to mind. We go to it clockwise, so everyone who wants to recite, can." The Capitan nodded encouragingly. Next to him, his daughter, Sheema, sat with her hands folded on her knees, a solemn expression on her face. She had not said much that evening, deferring when it came to her turn to recite.

"Your meetings must go on forever," Farzaneh said, lowering her eyes again.

"Well, we all have lives outside tonight, but—"

"But the subject tonight is love!" Houshang Bahmanian started.

"And next week as well!" the Capitan said, bouncing onto his bony knees.

"Watch it, or he'll keep on quoting Hafez until someone stops him," said Houshang.

"Baba," Sheema said, patting her father on the shoulder. The Capitan resumed his crossed-legged position, his face beaming.

"You'll never stop me from Hafez!"

Maryam, who had been sitting next to Haji Khanoum, suddenly got up. She went and sat next to her mother, directly across from Farzaneh Soltani.

Zadi looked at her young daughter. Those bandages on her wrist glared back at her. Her little one seemed curious about the stranger.

"You don't have to recite anything, of course, if you don't feel like you want to," Zadi said.

Farzaneh gave a small nod. She looked up. "Attar?"

"Perfection! Yes! Immaculate! Attar!" The Capitan clapped his hands.

Reza Sookoot shook his head. "What did you put in his tea tonight?"

Houshang turned to Farzaneh. "May I?"

And he began.

I vanished in myself, not knowing where I was found.
I was a dew from the sea, in the sea, I vanished.
At first, I was a tiny shadow upon the earth.
When the sun shined, from sight, I disappeared.
No signs of my coming, and no news of my going.
My coming and going was just a moment, it seemed.
Do not ask me how, because like the butterfly
in the fire of my beloved face, I perished.
Your body must become all vision, yet blind.
How I became blind with full vision, I wondered.

"How can a blind person have full vision?" Homa asked. "I think Attar is asking too much!"

"This is a metaphor, and it means if you want to see your love, your God, with the eyes of your soul, you should close your apparent eyes. I mean your eyes." The Capitan pointed his finger to his own eyes. "Close your eyes to the material world, to the perishable wants and desires." The Capitan looked at Farzaneh for affirmation, and quickly asked, "What do you think, Farzaneh Khanoum?"

"That is true," Farzaneh said with a very humble voice. "I think Attar doesn't want us to blind ourselves, but to close the eyes of material desire. In fact, seeing the world's beauty and the intricate interconnection of material things is one way to see the presence of God."

"I like when Attar says, 'I vanished in myself, not knowing where I was found,'" Haji Khanoum declared with a puzzling look on her face. "I think I vanish in myself when I swirl every morning."

"Please take me with you, Haji Khanoum!" said the Capitan.

"Me, too, please!" Zadi said, not wanting to be left behind.

Everyone laughed.

The discussion continued until late into the night. They were trying to digest Attar's spiritual meaning and teaching. What it meant to be a dew and vanish into the sea, to be a tiny shadow and disappear under the sun. How to be nothing and, at the same time, part of the whole. This created a spiritual air in which everyone felt divine connectedness and oneness.

Just beautiful. Especially the explanations by Houshang, and surprisingly by Sheema, who, due to her knowledge of nature, life, and the interrelation between the elements, found an opportunity for self-expression.

At one point she was explaining with enthusiasm, "In reality, we are nothing in comparison to the universe. We are like a drop from the ocean, but at the same time, we are the ocean. We are connected to the ocean, to the nature, and to the universe."

"And to the God," Zadi said.

"Not more blasphemy!" said the Capitan.

"I think that's enough spiritual intake. Let's have some tea and Esfahan's *gaz*," Zadi suggested.

Chapter Seventeen

Despite Zadi's efforts, word had spread fast about Farzaneh Soltani. People wanted to know who she was and why she, who looked so knowledgeable and spiritually penetrating, had come to Argentina. Most of them liked her and wanted to be close to her.

Homa thought of Farzaneh Soltani. She had been in their room, finishing up another batch of paintings, the ones set on the *Shahnameh*, when she heard the old man, the Capitan, talking to Farzaneh. She had moved into the corner room next to them while they were at the market. Homa told Reza later that night what she had heard about their new neighbor—nothing of much significance, mostly about Hafez and Tehran, where the woman said she was from; but he had still grilled her on every detail.

"She knows things, Homa. I don't know how she knows, but I know she does."

He paused, the small brush they used for painting facial features onto the people in the miniatures—usually princes and their supplicants—held up in the air.

Homa did not know what had gotten into him, but the years she had spent with Reza had taught her to read him well. He was terrified by the new tenant.

Zadi remembered her conversation with Farzaneh the morning after the poetry reading. Farzaneh had opened her door as soon as Zadi had knocked.

"Thank you, for last night," said Zadi. "For what you did."

Farzaneh looked at her. "I didn't do anything."

"But of course you did," Zadi replied. "I know you have your reasons. But what you did last night when you came into the poetry meeting—it was immense. How you changed everyone just by your presence. I thought they might have recognized you."

"People don't often catch on to the obvious—if there's no need for them to."

Zadi nodded. She looked up. "Your name. You didn't change it. It's your mother's maiden name." She blushed. "I remember reading about it."

"It's the one thing I could not bear to throw away," Farzaneh said, opening the door a little wider.

Farzaneh went to the kitchen to make them a cup of tea; since she had arrived, her daily commute had been this path to the kitchenette and shared bathroom, where she had nearly walked in on one of the women from the salon more than once.

She had glimpsed them working—shampooing or instructing a client on some treatment. The strangeness of these reminders of the hammam, in such a different form, was exhilarating. She had not expected to feel something akin to joy, but there it was. It was joy she felt when she had seen them in there, going about their daily practice.

And yet she had feared walking past the salon, and the other doorways, with their glass walls and curtains often flung wide. The women at the refugee center by the river, where she had been sent on her arrival in Argentina, had warned her of the curious setup at the Anna Karenina. She had thought they must be exaggerating when they told her the walls were made of glass—thought it in fact to be a euphemism for the gossipy environment—and so had been somewhat shocked to discover that they had been quite literal with the truth: the walls were made of glass. Stones and glass houses. That should teach her.

She had decided to give herself some time before looking for work. It was the sort of thing the refugee center liked to hear, but she had promised to give herself this, if nothing else. A time to breathe like she had never given herself before.

This morning, and after the last visit by Zadi, she had woken to a decision. She was going to make tea. She was going to make tea, and she was going to carry it up to the roof of this strange building. But when she got to the kitchen there was someone in there already, one of her neighbors whom she had not met.

Turning back, she had left the corridor and gone to the landing, where she had spotted the steps to one side of the far wall. They led to a hatch door, and the rooftop.

It was a warm day for that time of year, and it was comfortable there. There was a plateau wide enough for sitting. She perched herself there and looked out.

The many stone roofs of this city, the beauty of the green metal and the terracotta, made her think of Paris, and also of other places.

She leaned back and thought of that day with her baby daughter in a train from the north to Tehran.

Her daughter was just under eighteen months, her fat baby cheeks flushed like pomegranates. Farzaneh had cradled her to her breast, pointing to the sights outside the window, smelling the sweet sleepy smell of her. The kind of happiness she experienced with her was like no other she had ever felt; the ecstasy of those moments when she was writing, when in an instant all the truth of the world was right there for her to behold, to own, and then to propel forward; that was a pleasure; that was unquantifiable, as much as it was unreliable. She had written about it a dozen times, that second when, under her dripping pen, everything came together, the madness became right, the pain of this world (our pain), became only a step to that other time, to the love that was surely coming for all of us.

The whole beautiful, damned, and stupid lot.

That one really riled them up; the newspapers called her a radical. A female rebel seeking fame.

But then there was her little Nazanin. The joy she felt when she was with her, holding her on her lap in that train or taking their walks like they did in the square in their little northern suburb of Tehran. That was a happiness that was sometimes too much to bear. Too perfect. Too right. The kind of happiness that made you stop thinking of needs, of the bodily hunger for food and sleep. Time would stop. It was like being in a paradise.

Her husband was, as always, so supportive. So encouraging of her cause. They loved each other. They were in fire, in flame, for each other. Had it all been a dream? she asked herself.

"What is it about today? I feel positively great!" the Capitan popped his head into the salon the next morning. "Ladies." He nodded courteously as he stepped in. He turned to Zadi. "Any changes in the little one?"

"No."

"Well, not to worry. She just needs more rest, that is all," the old man said kindly. "I will bring her my backgammon set. I am in the mood to lose." He grinned, stepping out of the salon. "You know, I completely forgot about the piece I was going to bring for poetry night." He bounded down the corridor. He had forgotten the *Divan of Hafez* and his choice of poems.

The old man was happy today, thought Zadi as he disappeared from sight; this was the third time he had stopped by in as many hours; he had not even minded when he was addressed by some of the salon's clients.

"I wish I could come to the poetry night, too. I want to be there for Farzaneh. But Jamsheed . . ." Parastoo stopped herself.

Zadi gave Parastoo a sympathetic smile. She had never met Parastoo's husband, but from what she could tell, he was not happy about Parastoo's new job as Zadi's assistant. The assistant seemed reluctant to talk about her life outside the salon, so she and Haji Khanoum had kept their questions at bay.

Parastoo was remembering her argument with Jamsheed a few days before.

"That Zadi Heirati is a whore. Ask anyone who knows."

Jamsheed reached for another slice of bread. He used it to sop up the remaining stew on his plate, then resumed talking.

"I'd go and burn the place down myself if we didn't need the money."

He chewed loudly, sucking his teeth between swallows.

Parastoo sat across the small table from her husband. Lunch was nearly over. Just one more gulp.

Jamsheed tore another piece of bread and stabbed his plate. "What she needs is someone to really give it to her. Clear her out of any notions."

Parastoo stared into her tea. She could feel him looking at her, waiting for a reaction. Finding the right words to answer was the hard thing; whatever she said inevitably was turned on its head, misinterpreted according to the mood he was in. Besides, she was used to him talking like this. Always about destruction.

"Big shipment today."

"Oh, well that's good. Hopefully . . ." She regretted the words as soon as they left her lips.

"Hopefully? What's wrong with you?" Jamsheed's eyes bore into her as he leaned over his plate.

"I just . . . I meant that it would be good, for hope. For our future."

"I know exactly what you meant. Suddenly you're the oracle of everything, eh? A few hours in that salon and you know the secrets of the universe, eh?"

"We need the money," Parastoo said, a little too quickly for her liking.

She picked up his finished plate and took it to the sink.

Had she had a moment to think about it, she would have looked out the window first, as though contemplating. Then she would have said it, in a voice of regret, about the money.

As a sense of last resort, as though she wished it weren't so.

Instead of how it came out, stilted and tinged with fear.

But that was what it was like talking to Jamsheed; she was always calibrating, thinking three steps ahead.

"I don't even know why I tell you anything." Jamsheed grimaced, staring at her in disgust. He shook his head. "Piece of shit."

Grabbing the newspaper on the table, he walked out the apartment door, slamming it behind him.

He would be heading to the café near the plaza, where some of the other men, the ones who had no job to go to, sat drinking bitter tea and smoking water pipes and cigarettes.

Parastoo let out a breath; she held on to the counter edge. Hold on, she told herself. For another moment.

But even that was the wrong way.

Dizzy, she sat back down at the kitchen table and laid her head on the cool metal top.

He had been so angry. The Algerian he had met at the café had put him up to it. "Sequined vests, like the kind on that television show, *I Dream of Jeannie*," he had said, as always, excited. The Algerian had contacts in the garment industry. They were planning on selling the vests at the outdoor market.

"They'll be the biggest fashion in all Buenos Aires."

Before these, there were the plaster statues of Greek and Roman gods and goddesses. It had been like living in a mausoleum. Jamsheed had to give them away to get rid of the inventory when they would not sell. And then, of course, there were the lizards. Toy lizards that they were going to sell by the million.

Except they hadn't. They hadn't been able to get to America; the revolution had forced them to come to this city.

"These Western children. They don't know quality when they see it," Jamsheed had said when the venture had gone awry. Boxes of toy lizards lined the walls of their small apartment. They had spent nearly all their money on that idea.

Parastoo sighed and lifted her head. What had Haji Khanoum said the other day? "Choosing a man is like reading the Koran," the older woman had said as they had been preparing for a band andazi client. "Just open it up and take the verse you want. The one that will help you survive."

Was Haji Khanoum right? Could it really be like that? Parastoo wondered. Could you really just point and know?

Could you just pick the right words, the right thoughts?

And even if that were the case, how could you know you were choosing the right one?

It was hard to imagine having that kind of power.

She certainly had never felt assured, whether it came to love or most anything else, for that matter.

Surely if she had that kind of knowledge, she would never have picked Jamsheed.

Not someone like him, not someone whose own mother had admitted defeat.

"He's soft in the head," his mother confided in Parastoo the morning after their wedding. They were cleaning up the remains of the night's party.

There had been a lot of mess, especially from the *sofreh aghd*, the wedding blanket, with its good-luck items.

"Jamsheed's been like that since the minute of his birth," continued her mother-in-law, a small, religious woman who wore a headscarf even to bed.

"At first I thought he was all *garm*, all heat and temper, like the great fire in our temple. I did not mind it so, thinking it was better to burn bright than let go of the light. Every Zoroastrian wants this for her child. But then I saw the fire was only a cover."

Here she paused, brought her right hand to her left forearm, her tired face folding into itself with pain.

A strained muscle, Parastoo later learned, the result of her son's hands wringing it again and again. He found no difficulty, it seemed, in laying his hands on his mother or five sisters, when his anger blazed.

Her mother-in-law picked up the large mirror that had been placed at the head of the sofreh.

She looked into it, frowning.

"There is too much of the other side to him. The cold, destructive force, the evil Ahriman. The one our great prophet Zarathustra warned us of," she said, as though Parastoo had no knowledge of their shared faith.

"Mind you, never outshine him, Parastoo. He needs the light of Mehr shining on him. He needs to be the peacock in your marriage. Mind I told you. Don't make yourself too beautiful, or you'll be sorry."

There was never any danger of such a thing happening, thought Parastoo; she could never be beautiful, no matter how she cropped her hair to match the style of Googoosh, the pop singer who had even Jamsheed salivating, or powdered her face with both European powder and *sefidabeh*, the white chalk foundation of her grandmothers' vanity days. She was still the same plain Parastoo, the little swallow with fragile black wings.

He was the dandy, the peacock at every party, every picnic, every celebration they ever attended.

Reflecting on her life with Jamsheed, Parastoo had a revelation.

No, she told herself. She would never have chosen someone like Jamsheed Etemadi had she known.

Chapter Eighteen

The Capitan had been first to speak of Attar.

"And so we look at each other. Each of us gathered here. Are we not holders of that truth, too?" He looked around the room. "We are gathered here. Look at us, will you?"

"Hello." Farzaneh Soltani stood at the door. "I don't want to interrupt . . ."

"Khanoum Soltani! Come in, come in."

"I'm not interrupting?"

"Come in, come in!" Zadi said.

For a long time, you left me with concern

"Well, Zadi Khanoum. That's Hafez," Farzaneh remarked and recited the poem:

For a long time, you left me with concern
Embrace strangers, but lovers you spurn

"Please, continue your discussion," said Farzaneh apologetically.

"It's the unity that moves you forward," said Haji Khanoum.

"Unity, friendship," said Zadi, nodding.

"It's what I've been saying all along. Unity!" Houshang exclaimed, passion in his voice. He leaned forward, his glasses sliding down his nose.

"But is it necessary? Was that what Attar meant, moving forward?" Reza Sookoot spoke up.

"The question you are asking, young man, is whether union with the divine is a motion forward."

Houshang concurred. "Yes, exactly. Isn't it more a matter of earthly love, real action that creates life?"

"Then there would be no need for poetry," Haji Khanoum said.

"I wouldn't say that, Haji Khanoum," said the Capitan.

Houshang scrutinized the air. "What was it about the butterfly and the flame—was it Rumi who said something about necessity?"

"Well, there is the Hafez . . . ," the Capitan said.

My heart is burning with love.

Reza looked up, surprised. "I don't know where that came from." He turned to his wife, and then looked back at the room. "Something to do with reality? My love for my wife?"

"I think your heart is anchored to the flame," Houshang said, smiling mischievously.

"Just like my heart," the Capitan said, smiling first, then he looked at the new tenant and said, "My apologies. We normally do not discuss our personal affairs in our poetry circle."

Everyone in the room laughed.

Zadi looked at the woman across from her. She was sitting still, following the unfolding conversation.

The Capitan continued with Hafez:

Heaven could not bear this wonderful trust,
that to a madman this honor was thrust.
What makes the candle laughing isn't a flame.
The fire that burned the butterfly is my aim.

"Yes, back to the butterfly and the flame."

"Well, clearly it is a metaphor for faith," said Houshang.

"But it's more than that," said the Capitan. "Hafez was trying to tell us that it's free will. A choice we are making."

"Completely the opposite to what your Margaret Thatcher is doing now, Haji Khanoum."

"Houshang-joon, I simply admire her chutzpah, that's all. There's something to be said for all that gumption."

"There's nothing to be said for it. Nothing to being greedy at all."

"Yes, but let's come back to this," Zadi said.

Maryam, who was lying on a small mat against the wall, was watching the conversation intently, her head turning from one person to the next.

"Always choose the spiritual over the physical," said Houshang. "It'll never leave you wrong. The material will lead you into trouble . . ."

"You're too young to be thinking like that, young man. You don't really believe that, do you?" The Capitan turned to Farzaneh. "Farzaneh Khanoum, what are your thoughts?"

"You know, I was thinking of those lines again, the ones we touched on . . ."

Reza Sookoot suddenly said, before Farzaneh had a chance to reply one way or another, "It takes the same root or impetus."

"It begets the other . . ."

Everyone turned to the little girl who had just spoken.

Maryam stood up.

"It's just like she says in the poem. If you are in love with the fire, you have to go to the fire."

Zadi felt the cry escape her. *Look at her,* she thought. *Just look at her.*

Houshang looked at Sheema Bahrami, who was looking at Zadi intently. "What do you think?" he asked her.

"Hmm . . . yes. That could be another way to look at it, the butterfly to the flame." Sheema paused for a moment before continuing. "Metamorphosis. Death begetting that which is necessary. Necessity. *Burn me, burn me, burn. Time after time, again and again.*" She looked up. Farzaneh Soltani was looking straight ahead.

"In any discussion about necessity, I should mention how Marxist theory deals with social reality, and—"

"Excuse me, young man," the Capitan interrupted Houshang, "but let's not talk about politics and those theories that never did anyone any good. Yes, I know my politics."

"You don't know what you are talking about. It's the exact opposite of such blatant materialism. 'Society does not consist of individuals but expresses the sum of interrelations, the relations within which these individuals stand.' Tell me how that's any different from Rumi. Unity, unity, unity!"

"You don't know the meaning of the word," the Capitan sneered, turning away from Houshang.

"How about a break, a cup of tea, ha?" Haji Khanoum intervened.

"I don't know, Khanoum. I don't know anything." The Capitan leaned back against his cushion and looked down at the carpet.

Zadi was concerned. The Capitan had been acting strangely all night.

"Yes! It's a good idea. Tea is always good," Zadi said, starting to pour tea for everyone.

"I know my politics." The Capitan was thinking about his argument with Houshang, the words *politics, necessity,* and *reality* and Sheema's interpretation of the butterfly and the flame. His thoughts drifted back to his time in jail, which he had planned to tell Haji Khanoum about later.

. . .

Yes, the Capitan knew his politics. His knowledge had come at a high cost. After being in jail for many years, the Capitan received a letter and a photograph from Sheema, his beloved daughter. For him, it was a picture of horror. His daughter, now grown into a tall, thin young woman, dressed in a dark mantle. It was her wedding day, only a few months before. She was twenty years old. The young man next to her was the son of a very well known Mullah, a very influential man who could get this letter and photograph sent to the Captain in jail. They were lucky to be alive, living in Ankara, Turkey, where this Mullah and his son had many followers. Sheema, in that letter, assured him that she would always be taken care of. He mustn't worry about a thing. Something stopped in the Capitan from that day on.

Something changed in him, something so pronounced that he could feel it as a key, turning within. He was used to spending his days and nights with words, used to believing in words, but when he read what was before him, the words that in that letter had brought life and death in such quick succession, there was nowhere for him to turn but inward, to that place he had never known.

He became an unknown. To himself. To his brothers. Instead of waking early with the slants of light that pushed through the small cell window, he lay in his bed until midmorning, his arms heavy and leaden. When one of his brothers spoke to him, he could only stare back, empty pockets in his throat and chest. He was dead, he knew it. And as for the poetry, well, it was there, but it made him feel like vomiting to hear it. He could not hear or read any words; they made him dizzy, so confused that he would teeter if he got up from his mat and walk sideways, as though there was no internal compass to guide him right. It became so obvious that even the guards began to take notice, ordering him to stop his delinquent behavior.

The threats seemed to have the reverse effect on him, for he began to laugh and scream, nodding adamantly that it was the right thing for him. His brothers, his fellow cell mates who had been with him since the beginning, could do nothing for him but watch, and when he did not get out of bed one morning, they knew that their poetry circle had come to an end.

One by one they each left the prison. The young man from Tehran went first, transferred to a work camp in Lorestan. It was said that his father had bribed an official at the detention center, for it was certain that he would have been sent to the firing squad otherwise. Like the Capitan, he had been sentenced for treason against the empire. The other two, a man around the Capitan's age and a young father of four who had been picked up from the streets after stumbling into a rally on his way home from work, each left within weeks of each other.

And then the Capitan was transferred to another part of the detention center, to an area that overlooked the small gardens, which would have brought him joy at other times but only sickened him now. He grew gaunt and weak, but did not refuse the water and food given him. Something in him continued to desire the basics. Even this knowledge was hidden from him. Had he been aware of his basic need for life, he might have rejected it for the sheer ridiculousness of it. Things could have gone on like this for some time, he supposed, until the inevitable, but they did not. Instead they were set to change by the most unlikely of agents—a man so nefarious he could have stepped out of the stanzas of the *Shahnameh*, as ever present and as evil as the devilish Ahriman.

He began to go mad. He had been in prison for twenty years, but now he was alone. He was surrounded by so many cells, like the boxes on the corners of a carpet. But he no longer thought about the beauty of those carpets of his youth, only about the people inside of them, the woven creatures he had spent so many years conjuring with thread without a thought to how they must have felt, trapped in those corners with no way out. He forgot that they had a purpose, that within those boxes, like in miniature paintings, there were worlds and understandings, and it was within the grander context, the grander story of the carpet that there was the meaning of everything.

He forgot what it was like to depend on the love and need of others, he was so lonely in that jail cell. What was that line from Nizami?

It is not love of the houses that has taken my heart,
but of one who dwells in those houses.

And so it was with his mind, and so it was with his heart. And he had been such a young man when he entered the prison. Only twenty-one. A few years younger than Houshang Bahmanian with his quotations from Marx and Engels to the beauty of dialectics (yes, debate was all well and good when you had no line to answer but your own). The countless arguments he had had with that boy about philosophy, the nonsense about the senses and such. The older the Capitan got, the more he knew for certain that the senses were as important, if not more so, than any given thought.

The senses were just as close to God as any other understanding humans were granted here on this planet—but try to tell that to a young radical such as Houshang Bahmanian. If it were up to Houshang, he would have sealed off that oak door a long time ago and declared mutiny on the rest of the apartment block—the itch to transform was still fresh inside; it seemed to have increased in the last few months, exacerbated no doubt by his indulgence in all that rationalism and by the news he was watching on Haji Khanoum's television set. Haji Khanoum was the only one among them to own a TV, and most evenings saw the tenants gathered around its buzzing face, exchanging their opinions about government uprisings, and now this war. That contraption had not stopped their weekly poetry meetings as the Capitan had once feared it might, but it did not help matters when it came to the young man's revolutionary aspirations. All that watching of news from the world they had left behind, it just left them all rattled, Houshang especially, he who continued to rant into the night about the good of the many—unity, unity, unity.

The reed wants to return to its bed, it seemed, any which way or how.

Anyone pulled from a source longs to go back.

The moment came during his morning walk in the prison courtyard. He had by this time acquired his shuffle, the sliding and stooped way that had continued to the present, a kind of anchoring that came from a weight somewhere in his chest.

His coughs seemed to come from this region, too: the start of the tuberculosis. They were short and sporadic and did not bother him at all. On the contrary, they enlivened him, these onsets; they perked him up ever so momentarily out of the weightiness and lethargy.

But even as he enjoyed such a reminder of life, he also relished the notice of death.

On this day, the Capitan was shuffling along the paved walk, a dusty way that led to the shrubs, planted that first year he had been in prison. He had been the one to plant them; it had been one of the only jobs he was given.

He remembered how he had admired the lush foliage and the flamboyant flowers, which simply existed to reach out to the sun, to be alive, to live. How blind he had been! To think that that would be enough.

. . .

He was walking when he looked up and saw a man he had never seen before. The man was in the customary uniform of the prison guards. A tall man, with broad shoulders and a set jaw, a sharp and aquiline face framed with thick, arching eyebrows. All his other features seemed at first glance to be ordered and necessary to perform the duty at hand, the occupation he was given, but upon further inquiry it was obvious that something was not right. It was something behind the eyes, a kind of trembling of the eyes themselves, as though they were spinning on infinite alignments, waiting, just waiting to stop somewhere.

The Capitan could feel them watching him, and suddenly felt very tired.

Tiredness was a daily part of his being now. The other prisoners could tell this about him and left him alone for the most part. There was such a sad air to him that no one wanted to be too close to him for too long; they were afraid of the infection it could bring. But this man did not seem to notice this obvious character flaw. He kept looking at the Capitan as the Capitan made his way slowly around the courtyard to the water pump, where he sat down.

The Capitan continued to shuffle his feet along the stony ground, his eyes never leaving the pattern of twin obelisks he was creating in the dusty earth. He had been doing this for quite some time before he noticed the two dark boots.

"You are the one."

Something in the Capitan stirred. It was something that frightened him.

"I've been watching you."

The Capitan looked at him.

The guard nodded. "There is something I want you to tell me." He cleared his throat.

Last night before dawn, they gave me freedom from all
suffering;

in the darkness of night, they gave me Water of Life
everlasting.

"That is Hafez," the Capitan said.

The guard leaned forward. "Yes, but what does it mean?"

"The mysteries of the heart, why it keeps on beating."

The guard spat on the ground. "No mysteries, my friend. What it is about is that other sex. The dirtiness. They are beasts of burden, aren't they?"

"Well . . ." The Capitan looked into those eyes. "That is one way of seeing it."

"What other way is there?"

"What do you think of the next poem?"

What makes the candle laughing isn't a flame.
the fire that burned the butterfly is my aim.

The tumult of words brought the blood rushing through him. The Capitan could feel the energy surging inside his body. "You know the next . . ."

The dawn of hope that was hidden until now,
will soon come out, since the night is ended.

The guard stared at him for a moment. "I knew you would understand," he said.

The Capitan felt a deep breath escape him. Before he knew it, the guard had grabbed his arm, pulling him to his feet. "You are eating with me today."

. . .

He told the Capitan about his wife. How she had shamed him, left him for another man, a neighbor of theirs in Hamedan. They had escaped, gone on to England before they could get caught.

The Capitan said something about the English. Phantasms of barbarians, dwelling in nether regions, if he recalled correctly. The guard laughed.

"Whatever you want, you tell me, and I'll get it for you," he said. "You are the man. You are my Capitan now." He laughed, slapped him on the back.

The other prisoners kept even farther from the Capitan after this.

Back in his cell, the Capitan looked at the brick wall. The book of divans. He had not touched it in months. He wondered if it was still there, if it had not been eaten up into the mortar of the place. It was possible. He had been, hadn't he?

And then it happened. He scrambled up, and before he knew it the book was in his hand. Of course, he thought.

The next time the guard came around, the Capitan held the book up between them. Then he let it drop.

The pages of the divans fluttered in the dank cell for a moment, and stopped.

And that was when the Capitan knew he had been right. The look on the guard's face said it all.

Not that that was the end of the debate. After having tea, Houshang shook his head. "The taking of our oil in Masjed Soleyman. Neocapitalism at its worst. The British—who do they think they are?"

The Capitan sniffed. "Young man, I could write entire volumes on the matter."

"That's right, Capitan. You know. You went to jail because of it. I mean, it's not like I'm a communist—although I admire some of communism's fundamentals—it's about the ghalb. Yes, I said it. It's ghalb, at the end of it. But it's clear that's not the way things work." He looked at Zadi.

"The way things work. Things work because they have a way," Reza said.

Everyone looked at him for a moment. Homa shifted in her place. Zadi looked at Farzaneh Soltani.

"How about some poetry?"

"To end our meeting, I would like to recite a poem from Forugh Farrokhzad," Farzaneh said. Then, passionately and with a poetic voice, she recited the entire poem titled "Another Birth."

My whole being is a dark chant
that perpetuating you
will carry you to the dawn
of eternal growths and blossoming
in this chant I sighed, you sighed
in this chant
I grafted you to the tree,
to the water, to the fire.
Life is perhaps
a long street through which a woman
holding a basket passes every day.
Life is perhaps
a rope with which a man
hangs himself from a branch.
Life is perhaps a child returning home from school.
Life is perhaps lighting up a cigarette
in the narcotic repose between two love-makings
or the absent gaze of a passerby
who takes off his hat to another passerby
with a meaningless smile and a good morning.

Life is perhaps that enclosed moment
when my gaze destroys itself
in the pupil of your eyes
and it is in the feeling
which I will put into the Moon's impression
and the Night's perception.
In a room as big as loneliness
my heart
which is as big as love
looks at the simple pretexts of its happiness
at the beautiful decay of flowers in the vase
at the saplings you planted in our garden
and the song of canaries
that sing to the size of a window.
Ah
this is my lot
this is my lot
my lot is a sky that is taken away
at the drop of a curtain
my lot is going down a flight of disused stairs
to regain something amid putrefaction and nostalgia
My lot is a sad promenade in the garden of memories
and dying in the grief of a voice which tells me
I love your hands.
I will plant my hands in the garden
I will grow
I know I know I know
and swallows will lay eggs
in the hollow of my ink-stained hands.
I shall wear twin cherries
as earrings
and I shall put dahlia petals on my fingernails.

There is an alley
where the boys who were in love with me
still loiter with the same unkempt hair
thin necks and bony legs
and think of the innocent smiles of a little girl
who was blown away by the wind one night.
There is an alley that my heart has stolen
from the streets of my childhood.
The journey of a form along the line of time
inseminating the line of time with the form,
a form conscious of an image
returning from a feast in the mirror.
And it is in this way
that someone dies
and someone lives on.
No fisherman shall ever find a pearl
in a small brook that empties into a pool.
I know a sad little fairy
who lives in an ocean
and ever so softly
plays her heart into a magic flute
a sad little fairy
who dies with one kiss each night
and is reborn with one kiss each dawn.

A divine silence permeated the room for a few moments. Tears began dropping down Parastoo's and Homa's faces.

"Thank you, Farzaneh! You made our night," the Capitan said in a low voice, still not woken completely from the deep spiritual rapture he had received from the recitation.

Haji Khanoum said, "How beautiful, but how could you memorize it?"

"I bet Farzaneh has memorized the entire divan of Forugh Farrokhzad," said Zadi.

Farzaneh confirmed this with a smile and blinking eyes.

Chapter Nineteen

"About what we were talking about the other day—about loss and purity." Parastoo looked at Zadi. "It happened to me. I realized something. I realized I fell into a vacuum, thinking I saw something light. Something good."

"Jamsheed?"

Parastoo nodded, winding the thread around her finger. "When I met him. That was at the Persepolis celebrations." She paused. "He was so beautiful. All dressed up as an ancient Sassanian. I couldn't believe he wanted me. And I knew that I was what he needed, what he wanted."

"*Lezzat,*" said Zadi.

"That's it! Lezzat—gratification." Parastoo nodded. "It was a way, and I took it. It wasn't until the night before our wedding that I realized how wrong I was. What a wrong direction it really was.

"That night and the whole month leading up to it, I knew.

"I knew that I had chosen wrongly. That by bowing my head and showing my sharm, I had locked myself into something that would keep me from really living. I am saying this now to you, Zadi Khanoum, like I had a choice. But that is not so. Not for me, not from that first day at Persepolis. My father had no choice, either, he said, when he made me pack my things and move into Jamsheed's mother's house, where I was to stay as I prepared for our marriage. The deal was done, the pattern picked out, sewn up.

"Jamsheed wanted nothing to do with the wedding preparations. I made my own wedding dress, arranged the guests, the food, everything. He would only need to show up. He showed up all right, an hour late and with the smell of Russian vodka on his breath. The whole night, from the aghd ceremony, where sugar was sprinkled over our heads for a sweet life ahead, until our ceremonial green belts were sewn together, to represent our holy union, he was drunk and red faced. At one moment, he even tried to alter the traditional vows, in which I as the bride was asked three times if I wanted to take Jamsheed as my husband. It is customary, taarof, as you know, to refuse the first two times the priest asks, and merely to nod softly at the third. But Jamsheed would not even let me do that. After my second silence, he jumped onto his knees and clapped his hands, saying, 'Well, I guess that's it! She won't have me! But how about asking me if I'll have her, eh?'

"The priest was speechless. I was so embarrassed. I could see my father, across the sofreh, fuming under his white cap. I don't remember him ever speaking to me again.

"And afterward, when we had retired to the small room his mother had offered us in the basement, Jamsheed showed me my true self. I was sitting on the mattress, my heart flouncing in my chest, nervous to look up from my satin-covered high heels.

"He took one look at my face and grimaced. 'You are ridiculous, you know that? Take that garbage off. I never want to see you wearing such trash on your face again.' He licked his thumb and leaned over, drawing a wet finger across my made-up forehead. 'You don't think I know you are as black as the rest of us? That you come from the desert, too?' He laughed, an ugly laugh. 'You think you can fool me? Jamsheed, the Sassanian?'

"My white skin was my one attractive feature, I thought, for Jamsheed. I remembered how he had praised it that day at Persepolis, saying how it was as white as the Alborz snow. Every woman I had known, growing up in the desert, had wanted skin as white as the Alborz snow. Skin to match what a Persian beauty should be, apple-cheeked and pale, black hair and lips as red as pomegranates. And what nature hadn't provided, we provided ourselves, with powders and sefidabeh covering the darkness. Now this truth was uncovered, what I thought to be my only chance at beauty was shown to be a fake, a result of well-placed powder. And Jamsheed had known, even from that first day."

Parastoo stopped talking, and a few minutes of silence prevailed; no one wanted to say anything. They had been deeply affected by the story of her unfortunate marriage. Silence until she looked up from her henna application and said, "Haji Khanoum, I think you should tell us more of your story."

"Why, you are a hungry little bird, aren't you?"

"The morning following my birthday, Faezeh, my nanny, and I woke up to an empty house. I had not let her comfort me the way she had wanted to. I had pushed her away when she came to rescue me from my crying after my father's punishment. Now we came downstairs to the dining room. There was a letter from my father. He was going to Mecca, he wrote. He had left instructions and money with the overseer of the estate—Faezeh was to use it to sustain us until the day he should come back to this den of sin. When that would be was God's guess, or, as my father put it, *'It is what it is.'* You will know when you will know.

"The six years my father was gone were normal enough. I continued to be looked after by Faezeh, attending the local American school and playing like any little girl would. At nighttime Faezeh kept me warm with her back rubs and strange stories.

"I grew up, going through the stages that would bring me to the brink of womanhood. To the age of fifteen. To the day my father returned from the holy city of Mecca.

"As I have told you, many years later I would also see Mecca. I would drink from the Zamzam Well, which the angel Gabriel himself had dug for water, and walk seven times around the *Kaaba*, declaring the *Shuhada* over and over again. What a moment it was for me! What a joy to continue that circle. I would learn to stone the devil away in the town of Mina, seeing again and again how his will manifests in so many ways, is remembered and recollected in so many manners. I would become a Haji, aware and proud of the responsibility it would bring me.

"At Mecca I came to know peace. And so had my baba, it seemed.

"There he was, dressed in his *ihram*, the white Haj robe. On his feet were dusty sandals, and his beard was the proper length, unshaved.

"'Daughter,' he said, kissing both my cheeks. 'You are as I imagined you to be.' He turned to Faezeh. 'As are you, dear sister Faezeh. You have not changed a bit.'

"Clasping his hands in front of him, he gave us a big smile. He looked very pleased. 'Today for you is like the day of *Ghiyamat*, the day of reckoning. The beginning of what will be your new life, my Nikki. From this day on, my daughter, you are going to embark on your real womanhood. Faezeh.' He turned to my nanny.

"Faezeh swallowed hard. 'Agha.'

"My father tisked. 'Na, na. It's Haji now. No more mister or such.' He pulled out a coin purse and placed forty rials on the dresser.

"'Tomorrow, you will take Nikki to the hammam. The one near the park. Ask for Khanoum Abadi. She will take care of things from there.'

"I finally found my voice. 'Baba.'

"'Yes, my beloved?' My father grinned.

"I didn't know what to say. Did he even realize we had not seen him for six years? There were so many questions to ask. 'Baba, we . . . we don't know where the hammam is.'

"'Of course you do. Faezeh remembers.'

"Faezeh made a sort of squeak beside me.

"'But why do we need to go to the hammam? We have a bathtub here.'

"'No questions. Now you shall listen. You will take your pure body down to the hammam and get it ready.'

"'Ready? For what?' I could feel the lump in my throat rising. Suddenly, I felt like screaming. Like crying.

"'For it to be consecrated. To be unified in the only way it is intended. To be joined to another.'

"Faezeh began to whimper. She understood what my father meant.

"The 'another' my body was to be unified with was a man, Seiyed Faraodin, a Mullah. He was leader of the local mosque and a widower. He was also seventy-two years old. Apparently he had made his fortune in the carpet industry and, after his seventh trip to Mecca, was fishing for a new wife. Our cook told us all this when she brought our lunch later that day.

"'They call him the Spooner,' she said, placing the platter of saffron rice on our sofreh. 'And it's not what you think. It has nothing to do with his sleeping habits.'

"She scooped some pickle and chicken salad onto a dish. When she was done, she lifted the spoon in her hand and turned it.

"'See this back part of the spoon? The rounded end? That's what he likes to press into the arms of every wife he gets. The spoon treatment. He orders his cook to heat it up in the kabob oven first, of course.'

"She took another plate and set to work again. 'He likes to brand his women. That's what it is,' she said, shaking her head.

"Faezeh gasped and brought her hands to her mouth.

"I kneeled at the sofreh. 'How many wives has he had?'

"'The city lost count some time at the turn of the century. It's not like he keeps them for long anyway.' The cook saw the confused expressions on our faces. 'Temporary marriage. He marries them for a few days, maybe a month or two if the girl is something to really enjoy, then off he goes to the next.'

"'He can do that?' Faezeh was as oblivious to the idea as I was. As I've said, she was a simple creature, Faezeh. But she had a heart as big as the sky itself.

"'Of course he can do that! Men have been doing that kind of thing for centuries. Instead of marrying a poor girl for life, they get their kicks and that is that. Funny thing is, most times the girl is the one to suggest he marry another! Can you believe this?'

"Neither Faezeh nor I had the strength to look at each other. We simply stared at the sofreh, speechless the both of us."

"That night no stories were told. I lay in bed, staring up at the ceiling, a thousand thoughts pouring in and out of my head, none of them sticking. On the floor, Faezeh sniffled, in between prayers I had not heard her say in many years. All I could really see was the face of a giant spoon, a red-hot face pushing itself into my skin, leaving a half-moon burn to mark me for life. I must have fallen asleep despite those thoughts, because when I awoke Faezeh was standing over me, wearing a chador and veil.

"A few years earlier, the Shah had made it a law for women not to wear chadors. I remember our cook told us, her eyes bulging, 'The Shah has ordered every chador to be removed!

"'Every woman has to go bareheaded or she will be arrested!' She placed a pot of lamb stew on our sofreh. 'Police even tearing the veils from women who are defiant.' I could see tears running down her fat cheeks. 'We are doomed! Doomed!'

"Well, we were hearing stories about chadors from then on. The way our cook put it, it sounded like the whole country was falling apart. A woman without a veil, she used to say, was not a woman at all.

"Of course my father was completely against such an 'act of Shaitan,' as he called it, and ordered us to wear chadors no matter what.

"'Haji Agha! They are going to arrest us, the Shah's guards. We can't be wearing our chadors like this,' Faezeh reminded my father.

"'Let them arrest us,' my father replied. 'I want to see them try, the bastards. I will follow you to the hammam, and I'll be right across the street waiting for you to come out of the hammam when you are finished.'

"'Cook's made up some cheese and bread. We'll get the rest of the food at the hammam,' Faezeh said.

"Faezeh pulled me off the bed and handed me the chador. 'Your baba's outside. He's walking us to the bathhouse.'

"I stayed silent as I wrapped myself in the chador and drew the veil around my face, keeping it in place between my teeth, then followed my nanny to my fate.

"That walk to the hammam was like a death sentence. Everywhere around me there was life blooming. Second blossoms on the trees, and the crowds getting their shopping done before the holy day. Faezeh was holding my hand, and I remember the sweat between our palms running to the tips of our fingers, dropping slowly onto the ground."

"When we got to the hammam, my father said, 'I'll be right across the street in that coffee shop. Remember to ask for Khanoum Abadi. She knows what needs to be done.'

"The darkness and smell of perfume inside the hammam was enough to make me faint.

"Khanoum Abadi was waiting for us at the entrance to the locker rooms. She was a small woman, with a pinched look like vinegary pickles, *torshi*, across her thin face. 'Which one of you is the bride?' she barked.

"Neither of us replied. 'Never mind. Come, you are both getting the treatment anyway.'

"She pointed to two lockers. 'Put your chadors in there. First thing is getting your bodies ready for the band andazi and plucking. Five dips in the hot pool, five dips in the cold. I'll be back to take care of everything.'

"She walked away, leaving us to it. Faezeh and I sat down on the benches in front of our lockers. All around us women and girls were getting dressed and undressed. None of them were wearing chadors, not even headscarves. I tell you, I think it was more shocking to see them without headscarves than to see them naked. Faezeh and I remained in our chadors, unable to move for a few minutes. Finally, my nanny turned to me.

"'I am not going to let this happen to you, Nikki Khanoum,' she whispered. 'You can't get married to this man.'

"I shook my head and shrugged. 'There's nothing to do. It's done. As long as you come with me, Faezeh. I need you beside me,' I said, feeling a tremble rise through me.

"'I will always be beside you, little one. But it is you who must go.' She got up and walked to an open locker. Its owner had gone into the adjacent warm room and had left its door ajar. Faezeh came back and thrust something into my hands. 'Take these clothes. Get out of the chador now. He'll never recognize you without it.'

"'What are you talking about? I can't! He'll see me. He's across the street.'

"'Trust me. He won't know it's you. Now, do what I tell you!'

"I shoved the clothes, a patchwork skirt and long-sleeved shirt, toward Faezeh. 'No. I can't. What about you? I can't leave you here.'

"'Don't worry about me. I know where to go.'

"Faezeh gave me a parcel of bread and cheese and then pulled out the little purse she always kept in her large pantaloons. 'Take this. There's enough to get you to the Caspian. Take a bus to Tehran, and from there go on the train. Go to Bandar Shah by the Caspian Sea. Your aunt is living there. Find her and ask her to help you find a way to get to your maman.'

"'But I don't even know where she is. I can't,' I said, tears beginning to pour down my face.

"Faezeh closed my hand over her purse. 'Yes. You can. You can do anything, Nikki. You are that strong. I've known it since you were born. Since the moment you came out of your maman. I was there, remember?'

"I sniffed. She sat down next to me. 'All you did, as soon as the midwife pulled your head out, was look around. Those round eyes of yours, staring, staring at everything. Curious. Wanting. That is your destiny. This is the moment, azizam. Take it!'

"I did. I took those clothes, and I put them on. The patchwork skirt and long-sleeved shirt. The sandals too big for my teenage toes. And then I walked out of that hammam. Walked away from my beloved nanny, Faezeh. I could see my father across the street. He was smoking a *ghalyun*, with a group of men dressed similarly to him. He was nodding, but kept watching the hammam door. For one moment I thought to bow down and hurry, but something made me look up and straight at him.

"Faezeh was right. He didn't recognize me. He threw me a look of disgust and continued to puff at his pipe, never realizing that it was his daughter who was walking away on that street."

. . .

"The bus from Shiraz to Tehran crossed vast plains, cities, and towns that Faezeh had talked about, but I had never seen myself. The train to Bandar Shah went over new tracks, freshly nailed to the grounds of mountains and valleys. It was one of the newest routes, the ones the Shah had built for his new Iran. I saw the Zagros Mountains, beautiful valleys. My hair blew in tangles of black behind me, free from any hindrance as my nose took in all the fragrances of the open air. I knew water wasn't too far away when I felt the scent of salt and jasmine whipping my face.

"The ticket I had bought at the train station in Tehran was one-way to the coast, to the town of Bandar Shah. I had not known to stick it into the little metal window until the ticket master walked by and showed me how to do it. He was wearing a brand-new uniform and cap, just like the ticket masters of any European railway. He looked at my uncovered head and smiled.

"'Lustrous hair like yours should never be hidden under coarse fabric. I am happy to see you are of understanding, young lady. You know what the Shah wants to do for the women of this country.'

"I smiled back, pleased with his comment. This uncovering was wonderful, I thought. I felt like I did when I was young, before my mother left forever for Paris and everything changed.

"I felt free, yes, but it wasn't just because I was out of that house, out of Shiraz. It wasn't even because I had no chador or rusari on my head. It was because I understood what Faezeh had said in the hammam. She was right. It was my destiny to want. And all I wanted at that moment, there in that train, was not to think at all.

"The train rounded a forest, and then came to a stop. I leaned over and asked the woman and man sitting across the aisle where we were. In Behshahr, they told me. Two more stops before Bandar Shah and the Caspian Sea.

"I looked out and saw a little station house surrounded by bushes flowering with jasmine. Without thinking twice, I quickly got out of my seat and was down the aisle, out of the train. I did not know why I had left before the Caspian, did not know why I decided to stop at Behshahr. I just knew those bushes of jasmine had something to do with my new quest. This destiny I was following.

"There was no one at the station house window. It was closed for the day, a sign said. So I walked out onto a nearby road and followed a rocky path that went downhill to a main street. Above me, rising into the sides of a mountain, were the clay buildings and homes of a small village, one on top of each other so that one line of roofs marked the street of the next line of houses. The air was fresher than I had ever smelled it, thin and carrying the fragrance of jasmine. So different from the heavy clouds that followed you wherever you went in Shiraz, the beautiful but dark roses of my hometown.

"I passed the main street, which was very quiet, it being after trading hours, and walked down a wooded path. I could hear water somewhere, but was sure the Caspian was much farther away. The couple in the train had said it was two more stops.

"Suddenly, I came to a clearing and saw the river. It was wide and bordered by looming cypresses. I could hear the song of nightingales in the trees. And then it hit me.

"I was a fifteen-year-old runaway. I was in the middle of nowhere. I had seventy-nine rials to my name. And the ocean—where was the ocean?

"Oh! Ladies! Thatchers! What a cry I had!

"I cried and cried. For myself, for Faezeh. Where was she now? What had happened to her? How could she have sacrificed herself to let me fly? And how could I have let her? I cried for my mother, whom I had locked up in one corner of my heart, knowing she had gone and left me all alone. And yes, I even cried for my baba. For the strange ways by which he thought he was showing me his love, by marrying me off.

"I cried until there were no more tears to shed, then I dried my face and knelt by the river. The reeds in their beds sat rigid in silt and water. I took off the stolen sandals from my feet and waded in, weaving in and out of the thick green shoots.

"I remembered a poem I had heard Faezeh recite one day. My lovely nanny was not intelligent in the book sense, but she had memorized so many beautiful poems. And this was one of them.

> *Listen to the story told by the reed,*
> *complaining of being separated.*
> *Since I was cut from the reed bed,*
> *through me, everyone has cried.*
> *I have a burning desire to tell,*
> *the story of my painful yearning.*
> *Anyone pulled from his base*
> *longs to go back to re-join again.*

"I was thinking those words, and somehow they had sounded out into the air. I could hear them rising above me. But no, it wasn't me who had said them. It was another voice, coming from the field beyond me, from the banks of that river.

"I whirled around. There he was. Standing in the clearing. His long brown hair was flapping in the wind, hitting his face. Even from where I was standing I could see the green of his eyes—they were the same shade as the reeds I was surrounded by, and just as direct in their intention.

"'Not the best place to take a bath,' he said with amusement.

"My heart was beating madly, yet I could still find some spice on my tongue. 'That's how much you know,' I replied to this stranger, this man, this one. I lifted the hem of my skirt up to my knees. 'I was only getting a drink of water.'

"'By no means let me stop you.'

"I could feel his eyes on me as I stooped to the water. I had to let go of my skirt to cup my hands, bringing my face to my palms. The water was refreshing, smelling of those fresh reeds, but I could not enjoy it as much because of those green eyes. They were upon me still.

"I finished my drinking and looked back up. He had not moved from his place in the tall grass.

"'Why aren't you wearing a veil?'

"I shrugged. 'Why should I?'

"'You really don't know, or do you just want me to look like a fool? I'll happily look like a fool, if it comforts you.'

"I was thinking two separate thoughts at the same time.

"The first one was that I wanted this man to be inside me, that I needed to feel those eyes buried into my neck, into my breasts. The other one was that I needed to turn away, he was so beautiful, so divine in presence. I needed to run into that river and never look back. Without the want rising inside my belly.

"Ha! What thoughts for a fifteen-year-old virgin, eh?

"I did neither. Not then. I played with words a little longer.

"'You're looking like a fool already,' I replied smartly.

"Those green eyes twinkled. 'So that's it? You're not even going to ask? Don't you want to know why I think you should wear the veil?'

"I shrugged, there in the water. 'I won't give you the pleasure. And don't think just because you throw out some verses, I'll think you're a genius or something. The "Song of the Reed." As if I wouldn't know that one already.'"

"He stepped lightly along the grass. He was agile, despite his tall frame. I tried not to look at the triangle of skin where his throat met his chest, but I couldn't help myself. There was something so delicious about that browned skin, the hairs glistening with sweat. I could see his muscles move under his white shirt, and had to tear my eyes away with considerable pain. I could feel a pull in my stomach, something I'd never felt before. Suddenly I wished I was not standing in such prickly waters, realizing that if I were to faint, I would be stuck in the reeds, speared and caught. Suddenly I felt trapped with the rushing river behind me.

"The man chuckled as he approached the bank. He reached out his hand.

"'Come, there's no sense in sacrificing yourself for my pride.'

"I glanced at the river behind me. To unveil and run into the unknown was one thing, but to touch a man? A stranger? Now that was courage. I looked at his hand. And happily took it.

"His name was Jalalladin Ansari, he told me, as we made our way across the grass. He had been born on the other side of the river, in the woods beyond, but had kept his bare feet traveling from the time he had first grown a moustache. He had passed through African Sahara and gazed at a Siberian sunrise, eaten at the sofrehs of kings and shepherds. He had not stopped moving for fourteen years throughout it all, only temporarily to take respite at various ports around the world. All he needed in life, he told me, was the leather pouch that he carried on his back.

"'So my hands are free to welcome everything,' he explained, stroking his unshaven face. We were sitting under a cypress tree, my legs tucked under my long patchwork skirt. He was cross-legged across from me, running his thick, tanned fingers over the blades of sweet grass. My goodness, what a man! I remember thinking that I wished I had a veil, that I needed something to protect myself from myself. I especially thought this after he leaned over and pulled a blade of grass from my unkempt hair.

> *If you were a blade of grass, or a tiny flower,*
> *I would pitch my tent in your shadow.*

"He said, winking, 'That is Rumi also.'

"I smiled and bowed my head. He chuckled.

"'So you are in need of some shelter, yes?'"

"What was it about Jalalladin that made me trust him instantly? Why did I feel so at home with him? I still have no answer to that, joon-e man. All I knew was that I felt safe for the first time since my mother left me. So safe that I let him take me down the river, in a raft made of dried reeds itself. We arrived on the other side of the river and walked the path back to both our childhoods. As I abandoned any reservations I may have had, becoming innocent, Jalalladin was letting himself be led to the shack that he had been born in.

"The woman who opened the door was a copy of the man next to me. She was certainly as tall as him, strong and ruddy cheeked. She wore the traditional clothes of the area, and around her head she had a bright-scarlet headscarf. In her hand she had a mound of rue burning, as though she had already been preparing for her son's arrival.

"'Maman-jan,' Jalalladin said, kissing his mother's roughened hands. 'Ready as ever, I see.'

"'I knew a month ago you were coming. I already prepared your favorite meal. *Gheimeh*!' She turned and smiled at me in recognition. 'And this is she,' she announced, nodding. 'For you, little Khanoum, I have already prepared a bed. Come in, come in!'

"Jalalladin grinned and waved me to the threshold. 'Beware,' he said. 'She'll be reading your thoughts quicker than you have them.'

"I had never known a warmer home than the one kept by Khanoum Ansari. All that she owned in the world was contained in that one room, with its grass roof, and it was all that she could ever want, she told me as she prepared the yogurt and mint drink, the *dugh*, to go with our summer meal. Jalalladin had gone to bathe himself in a nearby stream while we set the sofreh. I had been in that hut for half an hour, but I was still finding things to marvel at. Every corner of the place was occupied by some beautiful thing.

"To the right was the cooking area. A little black stove filled with wood kept a griddle hot enough to boil a gorgeous gheimeh stew. The smell of lamb and saffron, softening in a bed of yellow split peas, sent my knees wobbling.

"I had not eaten since the day before, when I had gobbled up the last of the bread and cheese Faezeh had given me. Now I felt positively faint from the smell of that gheimeh.

"'Have a seat here,' Khanoum Ansari said, indicating to the sofreh on the carpeted floor. 'Have this glass of dugh. It'll ease your anxieties.'

"She handed me the glass of yogurt and mint water and returned to the pot of gheimeh. I took a healthy gulp of the drink, enjoying how it tingled as it hit the knob of worry sitting right below my chest. At once I felt better. 'Thank you, Khanoum.'

"'No need for thanks in this house. It is joy enough to give to you, little one.'

"An open window, framed with entwined bundles of twigs and curtained with a patchwork fabric, held a view of the woods beyond. I could see the sun setting behind the lower branches of the pines.

"'Khanoum, I hope you don't think me rude in asking, but how did you know I was coming?' I turned to the mat she had made up in the corner behind me. Another mat, bolstered by embroidered cushions, was laid out opposite. In between was another carpet, and more cushions, surrounding a small, carved tablet that held an ornate chess set.

"Khanoum Ansari laughed. 'I didn't know. But as the saying goes, whatever is in the heart will come up on the tongue.'

"I was confused. 'But I only arrived this morning. I only got off the train a while ago.'

"She stirred the pot of gheimeh and shook her head. 'I see it's going to take some time.'

"She walked to a small chest and opened it. From it she took three terracotta plates and a large turquoise-colored platter. She began to fill the platter with a combination of the saffron rice and stew.

"'Not everything has an explanation, little one. Let's just say for now that it was whispered by the *paries*, the forest spirits. There are a lot of them in the woods here, you know.'

"I must have looked pale, because Khanoum Ansari laughed again and said, 'Drink the rest of your dugh, little one. You're going to need a lot of nourishment before you are let loose again in the world.'

"The wind blew the scent of the Caspian in through the trees and window that night. It brought with it the smell of salt and caviar, and wild star jasmine. It was the scent of jasmine, Jalalladin said, that led him to his home again.

"'I've been to the hinterlands of Japan, where they serve it in tea, and to India, where it is laid out on a bridal bed, but nothing matches those small star-shaped flowers that border the sea just beyond these woods. They always remind me of my beginnings.'

"He smiled, reaching for figs in a bowl. He handed one to his mother. The other he gave to me, over the sofreh of fruits and tea.

"I was surprised I had the strength to take that fig from him. All night long I seemed to be growing more and more quiet in his presence, to the point that I had little mind to hold the hot glass of tea in my hands and had placed it firmly before me on the sofreh, afraid that I would spill it.

"Oh! He was beautiful! Those eyes, those beautiful eyes. They could have driven all the demons from the underworld with one turn of a stare, they were so pure, so light.

"Green like those reeds I had stood in when he pulled me out.

"'You are the best son I have,' Khanoum Ansari announced, taking a bite of the fig.

"'I'm the only son you have,' Jalalladin replied, amusement dancing across his face.

"'True, but you are still the best.'

"Neither of them tried much to engage me in their conversations. Rather they allowed me to sit and listen, watching the affectionate interplay of mother and son. But for the attentions of Faezeh, I had never really experienced such beautiful adoration.

"'Eat your fig, little one,' Khanoum Ansari said. Both she and Jalalladin were looking at me.

"I blushed, glancing at the ripened fruit in my hand. I remembered what Faezeh had once said about the fig, how it was Mother Nature's favorite fruit. I took a bite.

"Jalalladin laughed. 'I think it's time for the night.'

"He got up from the sofreh and crossed the room to where the mats were laid. His knapsack lay on one of them. He picked it up and undid the tie, pulling out something that looked like a web. It was a hammock, so intricate and delicately spun that it had fitted in his small sack.

"'Good night, Maman-jan,' he said, kissing his mother on both cheeks. 'And you,' he said, turning to me. 'Eat the rest of that fig.'

"He left the hut. Through the window I could see him recede into the forest.

"'He'll be sleeping with the paries tonight. He's happiest in the moonlight,' said Khanoum Ansari. 'As for you, little one. The mat is your welcome to dream paradise.'"

"The next morning, I awoke to the sound and smell of eggs cooking on the little black griddle. Khanoum Ansari was throwing herbs and spices into a large saucepan, mixing it all together. We ate, the both of us, as the sun came over the trees. I kept staring out the window, looking for the outline of the man I was already in love with, but it never came.

"'He's gone, little one. Already taken his feet to his next stop,' Khanoum Ansari said, reading my thoughts.

"'But he only just arrived.'

"'Arrivals are departures in the making. There is no difference between the two, in the end.'

"'But you haven't seen him in so long! Khanoum Ansari, he's your son.'

"'And that is why I can let him go,' she explained, scooping up the omelet with a piece of barbari bread. 'There is something you will learn about the men you will love, joonam.' She paused, straightening in her cross-legged position. 'You cannot hold on to them in any way. They must know they can fly. That the world out there is waiting for them. As are we, waiting. Here, with our windows and hearts open.'

"'But what if they don't come back?'

"'Well, then that is *Khoda*'s, God's, will. And following his will is the only thing a person, woman or man, can really hope to do properly in this life.'

"She paused, seeing the confused look on my face. 'Here, I will show you.'

"She drew an imaginary circle with her finger on the sofreh between our plates.

"'That is what women are like. Like circles. And this'—she drew a line—'this is what men resemble. The circle embraces and holds, because it is strong enough to do so. And the line must propel forward, because that is the only thing a line can do. Reach for the infinity a circle already knows.'

"She looked up. 'So you see, each one has their own duty to fulfill. That is how it goes.'

It is what it is.

"She got up, limber as a woman half her age. 'And now, we must proceed with our duties. We must do the washing,' she said."

Chapter Twenty

Would it be strange to say that I loved the man? the Capitan thought. *That within him I saw myself as well? How is this possible? But it happened. How close can man come, how easily, to fooling himself? I saw that the man was dead inside. I saw there was so little left of him—I wondered still how he did it, got up every day, put on that uniform of his and took to the corridors of that chamber of ruin. I saw what was there, and I was not afraid. At least not the way I used to be.*

"The fear came in a different guise. For I began to think like him—to imagine what he might see—and every time I did, I felt myself break in my head. It was a death, that kind of living. So easy to fall into it—to lose oneself—that I did not have to think like him in order to feel his anguish. It was easy enough. But what of it? How could this help me? I kept this knowledge within me, put it in a compartment, and proceeded with my plan.

"I could not even share this plan with my fellow prisoners. I did not know them very well, but I could still have approached them, I am sure. How I wish I had.

"And so what is it to be hidden? What was it to be aligned to something greater than yourself? To be in the dark but know that you are heading somewhere that is meant for something, that something that, yes, even Hafez, even Rumi were trying to reach and yet, yet that is what love is. That unknowable, that given, that sacrifice. To lose oneself in order to gain something else. But how did I come to this as a young man filled with need and passion? Ah, but I was not a young man for long. And to watch creation from afar? To see what a woman does in her body? To see what God does? Not seeing what I should have seen?

"Isn't that what fate is all about? And what is it to be a slave to fate?

"What to say and what to hear?

"What I did was for survival, and yet, now I know that I had little choice. No choice, perhaps. But still, it is not something I am proud of.

"I saw the worst in a mind—and saw how easy it was for me to become something of the like.

"Something of the kind of animal that was paying me too much attention, caring too much about the words that were not even mine to start with.

"When I thought of that man, I cannot help but think of what a ghost he was. Oh beauty, oh beauty that pervades—how it eventually touched even this individual.

"And so it is that we are all alike.

"And so I wonder all these years later as I begin to see the light at some other end, where all are called to *tawhid*, the unity with all existence, when is that moment, that one that breaks in someone? Is it something that happens before we are even born? When do we get pulled apart from our reed bed? When do we not long to go back? Do we or don't we all long to go back?

"My daughter says she is in love. That she must follow this path, down a river, with someone I do not know. She thinks I do not know, I cannot understand, but how can she tell me this? I only understand it too well. Down to the dust I am, Sheema, I want to say, follow your path, and I wish you the best."

. . .

"After some time, years really, that box, the cell, became comfortable. More than enough. The memory of my loved one, my beloved, the girl I had left behind in Tabriz, had become distant. Yes, even a man can lose his desire for a body and become something else—something close to divine. I did become happy. I reached a point where I remember the ground beneath my own feet seemed to hold me in a different way. When I stood, when I walked, I felt as though a rope was driving through me to the ground. Haji Khanoum says this is the divine—when she is whirling and feels this tug, this to her is the tawhid, the union, but tawhid can be achieved through other means. My mind was working in strange ways. I desired nothing but what was in front of me—and what I had was certainly not ordinary. The poetry. How could I not desire it? What else could I do? And so wars are waged.

"Had I lost? Had I won? I was no longer sure. Living in that prison had made me forget the things that were most important—for what is more divine than human love, than the want, the need to give to another person, to touch, to hold your daughter? This I want to tell Sheema now, but I cannot.

"She is studying the brain, Sheema. Once, I remember, she told me how we only use such a small portion of that mass—that if we were to use it more, the kinds of power we could have would be unimaginable. Dangerous, even. I don't want more than what is available to me now. I have seen what power does to a person. It is not for anyone to desire.

"Or are some of us so different, so separated? I wonder sometimes, and sometimes I do feel the pull, the remorse of having stayed on.

"To have survived.

"I said my daughter, Sheema, was braver than I could ever be, and I am right. Because she has always known. Perhaps I have always known who I was but I did feel like I lost something, was beginning to lose something, all those years back, during that time.

"I could not get away from the man. Everywhere I went, it seemed I was being watched by him. And there was something that happened to me then, too—it was as though I kept slipping in my mind, my thoughts. The further I went, the easier it was to let go of the moment before it, so that one thought did not always connect to another. So that I began to look forward to the man's visits. I even began to think of things I could talk to him about. Real things, not just the fates he was looking for. The ones that gave me so much power."

"There are ways to break a man that are not visible to the eye, and then there are ways that are so easy to tell.

"I began to see—I began to know how to make this happen. How to make this man come to depend on me. For everything in his day.

"So I told him what I wanted to see. I opened the book up to the pages I wanted. I had devised a weight in the binding that would allow this to happen. Of course, I could not do it all the time—he wanted some fortunes at the snap of his fingers, but I told him it didn't work like that. That he had to really think about what he was directing his will toward and that that took time—he would have to come to me with the right questions, at the right time. And that the next night we would find the answer.

"I felt like Shahrzad during her nights of storytelling. What a woman! The time it took me to find an answer using words already written—and she had to bring them up on her own, to have that courage. Courage upon courage. It is amazing, when you think about it. Some say she was not real, but what do they know?

"It was not long before I began to play with the lines of Hafez, discovering in them the fortunes he wanted me to tell. It became a cruel game that I could not stop myself from continuing. All I could see were the faces of my brothers as they were each taken away, never to return.

And the screams I heard. And I knew that I could not forsake them. That there must be a reckoning, that some things must be paid for.

"One time he wanted to know which prisoner was telling lies in interrogation. How torturous this was. Of course we were all telling lies. How could we not? But to lie about the truth is something else, and I could not sleep for the anguish. I finally found the passage. It was a ghazal about truth being the same as acknowledgement, as necessity. It did not stop him from picking out the prisoner whom he suspected had lied to him. He took this man, who I knew was involved with some underground movement, and had him beaten in the yard by my garden.

"The man died slowly, as the guard stood over him, reciting.

> *Bitter is this patience and so fleeting is this of mine*
> *How long will I experience this how long will I remain*

"The lines I had just given him.

"'See how this is?' he said to me after they had dragged the body away. 'Just like what we were talking about. The thirst that always makes them shout.'

"What was it about, that poetry? The strength of it that allowed this animal to embrace it? When he was capable of such cruelty, such insanity, elsewhere?

"Do you know what it means to play with somebody else?

"Do you really know what it means?

"It makes you feel sick inside. But it is also unstoppable. You hunger for it once you get the taste. Because it becomes the way by which you stay alive.

"Like the air, like water. Oh, I am ashamed to say it, to even remember.

"I thought, why was the prison built? What made it possible for us to accept such a thing? In a carpet, the purpose of the weave is the weave itself, and so it is with a prison. It exists because it exists.

It is what it is.

"So came the time when I could no longer face this man. I had to find a way of ending my own life. Or escaping it. I was going to die one way or another, I thought, but if I could escape, there would be hope for someone. My little daughter. My temptress of butterflies, my papillon. Something must be done.

"I came up with a plan. Finally the prison deemed that the men in our cell block should be put to work, that decades in prison for treason was too good for us. We were sent to a work camp on the side of the Alborz mountains. A dozen or so guards watched over us. We were instructed to dig trenches, but we did not know for what reason. In this part of the mountains, there was but one way to escape. Through the forest.

"I asked my guard to allow me to take a break. I said to him I wanted to smell the fir trees, to be reminded of what Hafez had said about holding forests upside down.

"My, how that got him!

"A break was granted, and he came with me to the edge of the forest. And there was my moment, a pocket, an opportunity.

"A suspension in all things that were real, that were sacred or not—this was it.

"I pulled out the book from the folds of my regulation shirt and let it fall. The pages opened to precisely where I had marked them.

> *Secure place and sweet wine and tender friend*
> *if only we could keep these three until the end.*
> *The world and its affairs are all nothing for naught*

a thousand times I have inquired of this trend.
Alas that until now I was so unaware
that alchemy of life is to befriend a friend.

"He did exactly what I thought he would do. He dropped to his knees and began digging.

"I thought if I could get to a stone, a rock, and pick it up, he would be gone. And I could run. I had just spotted my weapon when he began to put the dirt into his mouth.

"He was eating the ground, like a hungry beggar.

"'It is feeding me. This great love!' he said, laughing. 'Come, my brother! Come join this earth!' Dirt was smeared across his face and uniform. His eyes were wild with joy.

"I looked around. The other prisoners were half a mile away, moving down the trenches. And here was this man. Eating this dirt. And I knew that I could not go.

"He was going mad. And I chose to stay.

"This haunts me.

"As do other things . . ."

Chapter Twenty-One

Homa stood behind the stall, watching Reza bargain with a customer. The miniatures were beautiful, she told herself. They had been selling quickly the last few weeks, in spite of the commotion going on with the war. And she remembered a time when she had loved works of art and always wanted to be around them.

It was just before she had finished high school, before she met Reza. When Homa told her mother that she wanted to go to Tehran to study art, the history of it in Western culture, her mother had looked at her as though she had another eye growing out of her head. "You will do no such thing, and you know it. You will stay in Esfahan and marry, Homa. That is the only way we will get rid of this monarchy."

She was a very serious woman, her mother. She never liked to tell Homa bedtime stories like her friends' mothers did. There was only one story she would tell, and that was the one about Homa's grandmother. How she had come to learn the Koran by heart when she was only six years old.

Homa's great-grandfather owned a carpet factory in the city of Esfahan. Carpets were woven there by hundreds of workers, both women and men. One day her grandmother sneaked into the factory and buried herself inside a rolled-up carpet. This carpet was to be delivered to the local mosque, where her grandfather went to pray three times a day.

Homa's grandmother hid all day in the rolled-up carpet. She spent the entire time listening to the Koran being recited.

The next morning, just as a search party was raking Esfahan for her, the carpet was finally rolled out in the mosque. Her father was about to punish her for the trick when Homa's grandmother opened her mouth and began to recite the Koran. She had memorized what she had heard, entire sections of the book. The Mullah who was present was so taken with her that he made her father promise to bring her back to the square on Friday, so that she would recite it to those who could not pay alms.

Is it still a stone, or a world made of sunlight?

Homa often thought of her grandmother in that rolled-up carpet. She never met her grandmother; she died before Homa was born. Homa wondered what her grandmother was thinking while she was in that carpet. Was she afraid? Did the words she had heard comfort her? Is that how she stayed so silent in that cocoon? Did they anchor her, keep her safe?

Homa asked her mother, but her mother said she didn't know.

Her grandmother never lived to see the revolution happen. She did see another madness occur in their country, another hand played by fate and the American CIA. And when Homa's mother said that Homa's marriage would help to get rid of the monarchy, she was being her honest self.

.   .   .

Parastoo stood on the landing as Zadi came back from the kitchenette, carrying a bowl of cooling henna paste.

She had missed the making of the henna paste, thought Parastoo. She had missed it.

But she had said no to Jamsheed.

He had been eating his dinner when she said it. Though it had not come out the way she had expected.

"I am tired," she said.

He looked up from his plate, confusion briefly crossing his face. Then he nodded. "Then go to hell!" he laughed. "Go to hell!"

"Jamsheed, I don't like the way you talk. I am tired of it," she stood up from the table.

Jamsheed sneered. "Eh? Are you now? Well, I see I have to watch what I say then. Wouldn't want you to get tired."

And that was when she had fallen. Dropped right there in the middle of the room. He looked at her for a second, then returned to his dinner.

"You are bad to the core, Jamsheed. Do you think I'm stupid? Do you think I didn't know what you were doing, from the beginning?"

He continued to eat, shaking his head. He sniffed, as though pitying her.

The words came to her.

She looked up. "You are so ugly."

They were like magic.

So she sat there and had to decide whether she was going to live or die. She did not know when he had left the room or the apartment. But it seemed like hours before she summoned all her strength and walked out. She was dizzy, and did not even know where to look, what street to walk down. She just had to trust that somehow she would be guided to the right avenue, to the right house.

"I don't want it anymore. I can't anymore. Is that enough?"

"More than enough."

"But Jamsheed's voice. It's there. It's there all the time."

"That's Jamsheed's voice, not yours."

Yes, not mine, Parastoo thought.

The pack on her jaw was cooling. Zadi smiled, kindness in her eyes.

"You'll stay with me now, Parastoo-jan," Haji Khanoum said. "We'll make a real time of it, just you wait."

Zadi watched the henna leaves soak. The paste would be used for a bridal party that was coming in the next morning.

My beloved is unto me as a cluster of camphire, in the Garden of En-gedi.

She had once heard the Capitan say that one turning point, one moment, could change everything forever.

Had she not had many of those instances, moments in her life that had changed the course of things? And she had managed to get through them, to rise again.

Farzaneh took in a deep breath. The sun began setting over the rooftops. She watched it, remembering.

He had shared her vision, admired her purpose, and enjoyed her strength.

She thought of that winter they were together. They had gone to their cabin with a garden, in the mountains outside the village of Damavand.

She was standing watching him from the kitchen, the sponge in her hand. He was planting the bulbs in the small garden, for a time when they would no longer be there. She would have called him a fool, had she not known he was right.

Minutes passed before she realized she was just standing there. The glass she had been washing was still in her hands. There was a spot on it, where their mouths had shared the drink. She scrubbed it. And it happened. In that moment, in that simple act of standing there.

This was life, she thought, looking at the glass. And words came to her, first from Rumi, then from Forugh. Flying out into the yard, she yelled the words, inscribing them on the air.

> *I whispered in his ear the tale of my love:*
> *I want you, o life of mine,*
> *I want you, o life-giving embrace,*
> *O crazed lover of mine, you.*

Later, she drank a glass of warmed wine, watching his profile. He had dark hair that curled at his temples. His body was as lithe as a runner's, his fingers stained with ink and the dirt from that garden.

They lived and enjoyed every moment together, side by side, that whole winter, planting new trees, pruning old ones, and making their garden ready for spring and summer.

They held each other and whispered words of love.

She whispered "Another Birth" in his ear:

> *I grafted you to the tree,*
> *to the water, to the fire.*

And he whispered "The Ruby and Sunlight" in her ear:

> *I am so vanished in you,*
> *that I became totally filled by you.*
> *Nothing left of me but a name;*
> *nothing exists in me but you.*

"The days and weeks passed slowly and peacefully in that hut in the woods. I helped Khanoum Ansari with the daily chores, the slow and steady work that kept my hands busy. My mind, my heart, could not stop from spinning around those green eyes, to Jalalladin and the love that was growing inside of me. I did not dare voice my desire to his mother, but the way she looked at me, catching me gazing into those woods where his hammock had hung, I am sure she already knew my thoughts.

"I had not forgotten the words Jalalladin had said the day I had first arrived, when I had been filled with curiosity as to the nature of Khanoum Ansari's talents. Was she one of those fortune-tellers Faezeh always told me of in her stories of the *One Thousand and One Nights*? There were many such gypsies in real life, Faezeh had said when I asked her if there were people who had such powers to tell the future.

"'I have seen them myself, when I was growing up. They would come in with their caravans, all the way from places in the north. You know, a lot of ancients left Iran for colder climates. These gypsies were among them. Whenever they passed our camps, we would all go inside our tents and not come out until we could not hear the wheels on those strange carts. You have to be very careful with those gypsies, Nikki Khanoum. They don't only read your thoughts, they eat them.'

"'Eat them?'

"'That's right. They take your desires, your wants for the future, and put them in their bellies. It's like food to them. And then they charge you for their services,' Faezeh shook her head.

"'They carry some kind of wooden sticks, with which they see your life, your future. Just make sure you never come across them. If they pull out their tools, those sticks that tell all sorts of sorcery, you run.'

"'I can see you are wondering whether to run or to ask me about those,' Khanoum Ansari said one afternoon. I was standing before a shelf of curiosities. 'Come, I'll show you.'

"She took the sticks and sat down on the carpet. She indicated that I should take a seat opposite her. She then closed her eyes and took a deep breath. When she opened her eyes again, there was a shine to them. A faraway look.

"She then threw the sticks onto the carpet. They landed, some on top of one another, some separate.

"She looked at the pattern and smiled. 'Yes, just as I thought.'

"'What do you see, Khanoum?'

"She looked at me. 'Your destiny, little one. It will be one of the phoenixes.'

"She indicated four sticks that had formed a triangle, split in half. 'This shows that your life will be one of transformation. You will be continually resurrecting yourself from ashes. And in doing so, showing others how to be born again. To be strong again.'

"I could not see how she could tell all that from those sticks. 'Your path is a long one, little Khanoum. Be prepared. It will never be dull.'

"And with that she stood up and placed the sticks back on their shelf. 'Now,' she said, clapping her hands. 'Time to clean the pots and pans!'

"I did not want my path to be varied. I did not want to have ashes to rise up from. No! I wanted to stay right where I was. Safe and sound in Khanoum Ansari's hut. Doing my daily chores and waiting for that green-eyed son of hers to return. I had not been so happy in all my life. Why would I want to exchange that moment for the unknown, for the destiny Khanoum Ansari saw in those sticks?

"I did not ask her this, of course. To do so would be to spit in the face of her hospitality and kindness. And also to question her wisdom, which was great. I kept my thoughts to myself, and only entertained them at night, before I slept, while looking out the window. And then, one day, a few months after I first arrived at the hut in the woods, Jalalladin returned.

"And I found out that Khanoum Ansari's predictions were right."

Chapter Twenty-Two

The morning had been a busy one. The salon was filled to capacity, with every seat taken up with waiting clients. Khanoum Tapesh, who had come in again for band andazi on her chin, sat herself before Haji Khanoum and picked up where she had left off the other week, grilling Haji Khanoum about Christianity. In Parastoo's chair, another regular client was defending her decision to return to religion, which, to her husband's chagrin, consisted of alms to the mosque on Alberti Street three times a week. "I can't believe I've gone without such a touchstone all these years," she said as Parastoo touched up the roots of her hair with henna.

"And what of beauty? How important is it to everything we do, everything we are? I don't think without feeling that desire, I could be doing all this today," Zadi spoke up suddenly.

"You are a romantic, Zadi-jan," Parastoo's client said.

"Not a romantic. A realist."

Haji Khanoum laughed. "I was looking the other way when those two separated:

I'm the servant of the moon; talk of nothing but the
moon.
In my presence say nothing but of light and sweet.

Don't tell of suffering, say nothing but blessings.
If you know nothing about them, no matter. Say
nothing.

I'll whisper secret words in your ears,
Just nod yes and say nothing.

A moon, a pure soul, rose on the heart's pathway,
How delightful is traveling along that way, say nothing.

You who sit in this house filled with images and
illusions,
get up, walk out the door, go and say nothing.

"Now is the time for me to say nothing," said Haji Khanoum and sat down reflecting on the poem.

Zadi took a walk around the block, heading for the grocer across the street. Crisp autumn smells hung in the air, the limestone and red bricks of the old buildings shimmering in the afternoon. Although she knew she was on the other side of the world, it was hard to remember when autumn had been anything but this, washed in colors that were suspended, neither delicate nor strong. Penetrable but still indefinable.

A bridal party was due at the salon. She had decided to step out for just a moment, to see the open sky again.

She looked up. A flock of pigeons momentarily hid the sun.

. . .

As the dusky sky stretched across the atrium, and after the final cups of Darjeeling tea were drained, the women who had come to the salon gathered around the table in the middle of the room.

Zadi stood back, smiling.

She remembered something Khanoum Mina used to say: "Let the beauty you love be what you do. And the drumbeats begin playing."

"We had just come back from picking mulberries in the forest. They would be soaked in sugar water and then laid out on a blanket in the sun to become the dried *toot* that we all love so much. Such a tasty treat! I had a barrel of the berries in my arm and was following Khanoum Ansari when we both stopped short. Jalalladin was on a patch of grass not far from the front door. He was kneeling on the soft grass, praying. When he lifted his head, he smiled.

"'Maman-jan! We did it! The Brotherhood is together again!'

"Khanoum Ansari lowered the barrel she was carrying and clasped her hands in thanks. 'God be praised! This is a good day!' They embraced and did a funny little dance there in the grass. Khanoum Ansari waved me over.

"'Little Khanoum! Come and help us celebrate. We are going to have a feast today!'

"They walked into the hut, laughing, leaving me standing there with my mulberries.

"The Brotherhood was a band of heretics. We all knew about the Sufis since we were young, yes? The handful of soul wanderers who practice their devotion to the divine through prayer, teaching, and that dance of all dances, the whirl.

"Jalalladin was one such man. He had come home from his travels to unite a group of his brothers on the banks of that river where we'd first met. They had set up a camp on the river's bend, he told us, not two kilometers from the hut, and were beginning construction of a school, a building where they could teach and study in turn.

"'I put out the word when I was in the area. I never thought it would carry so far, and so fast!' Jalalladin was so excited that he could not sit down at the sofreh, but kept leaping up onto his knees, slapping his thighs for emphasis. His mother smiled proudly as she ladled goat stew onto the terracotta plates.

"'I'm being reunited with brothers from the Americas and Scandinavia. Even Houshang, the Knower, whom I had not seen since my school days. Remember him, Maman?'

"'How could I forget? He was the most talented of you lot. The most intuitive, I recall.' She turned to me. 'You think I can read minds, little Khanoum? You should have been there to see Houshang whirl. After one session, he could look into your eyes and spell out the exact moment when you lost your innocence, your ability to be a child. He was that good.'

"Jalalladin nodded. 'And still is. He's turned to healing now, Maman-jan. Been on the Spanish front for a while, part of the resistance there. He plans to go into the heart of Europe next year. He says there is a war on the horizon.'

"'*Inshallah* that is not true. Though even I feel it,' Khanoum Ansari handed me a glass of sugar water. 'You are being quiet this evening, little one. Shy to ask Jalalladin what is on the tip of your tongue?'

"I was about to ask her how she knew, but then remembered she knew a lot. I looked down shyly and shrugged.

"Jalalladin laughed. 'Out with it now. There's no hiding anything in this hut.'

"'What is whirling?' I asked, feeling very stupid for not knowing.

"'You have been tucked away, haven't you, little one?' Khanoum Ansari said. I nodded. 'That is all right. Better to be tucked away than to scatter yourself in the wind.' She pointed to her son. 'Jalalladin, tell your little guest of the turn, yes?'

"Jalalladin stood up. 'Ah, but to do that, we must go to the beginning. The birth of the tradition. And to do that, we must go to Rumi.'

"Jalalladin winked at me. 'I know you know this,' he said, referring to our first meeting.

"I blushed and looked down.

"'Yes, Rumi the poet. Rumi the man who started so many of us on our journey.' Jalalladin moved away from the sofreh. He positioned himself on the mud floor, his legs apart, his arms open wide. He swirled about, coming to a full stop after one turn. 'This turn, you see, is where it all comes to in the end. This turn, repeated over and over again. This is how we pray, how we reach a state of union with the force that is above us. Below us. All around. Yes?'

"I nodded, following every syllable coming out of his mouth. I was transfixed. With every word, I was falling deeper and deeper in love.

"Jalalladin continued, 'But in order to turn, you must turn with love. And that is how Rumi did it. Here now. Listen, little one.

O my heart, sit with the one who knows your ways,
sit under the tree that has fresh flowers.
Don't wander aimlessly in the bazaar of perfumes,
stay in the shop of the one who has sweet potion.
If you don't know how to measure and judge,
anyone can sell you false coin for gold.
Not every cane has sugar, not every chasm a crest,
not every eye has vision, not every sea has pearls.
Safeguard your glowing-heart lantern from the wind,
You must get yourself out of this stormy weather.
When you pass the storm, you will come to a fountain,

where you will find a spring of nourishing water.
When you are supplied with nourishing water,
You will be an ever-green tree with fruits forever.

"What followed were three beautiful months, the best I have ever lived. And you all know I have lived, yes? Such a journey, such a dance! But nothing I have ever felt since has come to match that time in the hut.

"Jalalladin came to the sofreh every night. After a long day working with the Brotherhood, he would come home to his mother and me, to a dinner around the blanket of our hearts. Every night he would bring us some more news, an update on how the house the men were building was coming along, how their plans were taking shape.

"'The foundations are set. Now we are putting up the walls,' he said one night. 'There is going to be a glass dome for the roof and a fountain in the middle of the floor. An eternal reflection going back and forth. What a place this will be!'

"I, too, began to look on him with proud and shining eyes, just as his mother did. I, too, began to sing and work steadily every morning and day, looking forward to the night. I began to understand what Khanoum Ansari had said about men. It was so simple, so right. To follow one's duty, to take it all in one's stride. To be a woman so unlike my mother. To love a man so unlike my father.

"Oh, God, I was in love! I dove into that ocean without even realizing it. Maybe I needed to. Maybe it was the right time for my heart to open that way.

"For his part, Jalalladin never showed me anything but the love and respect a brother would have for a beloved little sister. There was no sign in his eyes that he desired me with the same flame that I had for him. And I wouldn't have known that he had seen my want, that he knew fully what was whirling inside of me, were it not for one afternoon in late summer.

"All our duties were done for the day. The floor had been swept and the herbs bundled and hung out to dry on the branches of one of the trees outside. In the icebox, a clay belly dug into one corner of the mud floor, there sat chilling bowls of yogurt dip with tomato and basil, while a chicken had been roasted outdoors and then shredded and added to a salad of watercress and lemon mint for our dinner that night. As was customary during the hot afternoon, Khanoum Ansari and I had taken ourselves to the mats, where we would sleep before rising to greet the twilight and the arrival of Jalalladin. But this afternoon, I was not able to sleep. Khanoum Ansari was well into her second cycle of snores by the time I gave up trying to rest. My mind had not stopped working itself over since the night before, when Jalalladin informed us that the Brotherhood was nearing the end of construction of their temple. 'Another week and we'll be able to have two dozen whirling at the same time under its roof! Maman, I wish you could see it.'

"'I can see it, joonam. Your descriptions alone are enough for me to enter it with my mind, even if my body is not allowed.'

"She saw my expression, which was so often one of awe or confusion when she and Jalalladin spoke. 'It's for the Brotherhood only, the temple. No women are allowed to see inside, little Khanoum.'

"'Ah, but the temple of the earth is all yours, Maman. It is and always will be for the mothers.'

"Khanoum Ansari winked at me. 'I brought him up well, don't you think?'

"I did not have time to agree. Jalalladin was already out the door, his hammock slung over his wide shoulders. 'Only a few more weeks, and then I am gone, Maman. The cypresses are going to blow toward the west once more.'

"'And that is how it is, little one,' Khanoum said with a wistful smile. 'The cypresses blow, and they are gone.'"

· · ·

"I was thinking of all of this when I got up from the mat and made my way quietly out of the hut. I wanted to walk for a while, to take the path down to the river and those cypresses. To ask them, perhaps, if they would blow another way for once. Or demand that they stay still, so Jalalladin would as well. How could I let him go? How could I see him leave again, maybe this time forever? Khanoum Ansari might have been right. Maybe it was our duty to stay grounded, to spin our webs while the men went out into the wide world, but somehow I could not agree with it. Not anymore. I wanted to follow Jalalladin, wherever he was to go.

"I knew I was forbidden to walk north to where the temple was being built, so I took the river path south. I walked under the leaves of those cypresses, hearing their soft moans, thinking of the trees and bushes of my childhood home in Shiraz. I thought of Faezeh and how courageous she had been to push me out of that hammam, to make me run when she could not. And now I was welcomed into the arms and home of Khanoum Ansari only to plan another escape, with no gratitude. How could I be so selfish?

"The cypresses said they did not know, and that I should truly be ashamed of myself. I should turn on my bare heels and get back to the hut and my mat before Khanoum started her third cycle of snores. And I did. I turned. I took a step back. And then stopped when I saw Jalalladin, not ten feet away in the water.

"His back was toward me. And what a back it was, Zadi! Grooves and mounds of muscle, from those wide shoulders down to a trim waist. Dark amber in color, from the sun of so many of his journeys. And his hair, the dusky brown, wet, clinging to his neck.

"He was bathing. And he was naked. My Jalalladin, my one, my everything—he was completely buck nude. Ha-ha! What an education I was getting.

"I quickly hid behind a cypress tree and watched. Jalalladin dove into the river and came back up again, rinsing his hair. He had a bar of palm-oil soap in his hand, and he used it to lather his chest, which was now clearly visible to me. He slid it across his body and made it go down, past the trail of hair. My goodness! And then the soap stopped. And so did Jalalladin. He washed the rest of his body and stepped up onto the bank. Right next to where I was standing.

"'That dark hair of yours could be seen from anywhere, little Khanoum. Not even the cypresses can cast such shadows.' He knelt down to where his clothes lay, clipping them on before I had a chance to blush. 'Why don't you come out from your hiding and tell me what you saw?'

"I did not move. 'All right, if you don't move, then I'll come to you.' Jalalladin stepped up to the tree and pulled a lock of my hair in teasing. 'Now, what would Maman say if she saw you here, in the brightness of this afternoon? Would she approve, do you think?' He held out his hand. 'Come. Let me guide you to a safer spot.'

"I took his hand. I let him lead me toward the field beyond the bank, to the tall grasses that came to my thighs. 'Now, what were you really looking for when you came out to the bank? Surely it was not to get such an early start on making love?'

"I looked into his green eyes. I saw their kindness. And their amusement.

"He did not love me the way I wanted him to. But I could not stop from saying it anyway. 'I love you, Jalalladin Ansari. I love you and I want to come on your path. I want to walk by your side.'

"'Didn't Maman tell you that was not the way of things?'

"'Yes, but—'

"'There are no exceptions, little one. Love or no love. I love you, too, but it is not the kind of devotion that will make you the woman you are destined to be.'

"'But it is! You don't know.'

"'I do know. I know this is not what is right for you. When it is, you will not need to hide behind a cypress tree. You will take your clothes off and dive right in.' He smiled. 'But until that time, you must follow the—simple—path you are given. And to do so, you must learn to align yourself with a greater will.'

"He placed his legs apart, and lifted his arms. 'Yes, follow me. Like this.' He turned once in the grass. He stopped and nodded. 'Now you. Go now.'

"I paused. He nodded again. I lifted my arms like his. I turned.

"'Good. Now again.' I repeated it. This time I could hear the blades of grass bend beneath my feet. When I stopped, I saw there was a circle clearing under me.

"'Again.' Jalalladin turned, and I with him. 'Keep your right palm up, inviting the rays. Keep your left palm down, giving it to the ground.'

"I did as he said, as I turned and turned and turned. I kept circling on that clearing, kept going as the world and the river and Jalalladin disappeared. 'Hold on to yourself, and let go of your breath.'

"I did as he said. And I kept whirling away.

"I kept whirling. And I realized what Jalalladin had meant all along about the beloved.

"I had been thinking of it in terms of purely earthly senses, of the touch and pounding of our bodies. But that union is nothing to the one that I felt there, as I turned.

"'Once you have that knowledge, you can never be lonely again,' he said."

Haji Khanoum was out of breath. The memory of Jalalladin always did that to her. It was almost fifty years since that day by the river, and still she could see him as though he were coming out of the water, standing right there in front of her, his hair and chest shimmering in the afternoon sun.

Oh, that piercing, human feeling, that sheer desire that had not left her! For although she had understood his words then, had reached through to moments of understanding of what he had tried to teach her, she would still have turned all that knowledge back to be a woman with him. To be loved and touched by him as a woman should be.

Oh, he was never far from her thoughts. The only time she was released was during her whirling and that was something, yes. But one could only whirl for so long, and although she did not want to say it out loud, she knew that her time was beginning to end.

Of course, that was not what she had told the others. There was such thirst in them for something to hold on to, some kind of belief, that she could never bring herself to tell them everything. "He was beyond his time," she would say. "Not just a man."

Telling them that she still craved Jalalladin's touch, to see his body and smile again—those green eyes—what could be achieved by such a thing?

So whenever she was called on to tell the story, she would always tell them how she had believed Jalalladin to be right, that there was a greater way than the one she wanted, the romance she craved.

But that was not how she truly felt.

What could she do with what she had left?

Still, she thought, he took it too far. She could have been in bliss with him, could have needed nothing beyond it. He did not feel the same way perhaps. She would never know. Jalalladin's decision had sent her on a path she would never have chosen for herself. A path that had brought her to this place, this moment. To these people who were waiting to hear it. Even if they did not know it.

Now she must show them, her wonderful friends, what it was. She must show them how to grab this moment.

Chapter Twenty-Three

I wanted to be useful, to do something good for women who had been in disadvantage, thought Farzaneh.

Farzaneh Farahanguiz was born in Ghazvin and moved with her family to Tehran at the age of fourteen. At school, she found her interest in philosophy and in literature. She loved contemporary poetry, particularly the poems of Forugh Farrokhzad.

Forugh Farrokhzad, the most talented and most famous contemporary woman poet, a poet who had a unique gift which sprang from a deeper well, something special given to her by God himself. A talent like no other. She could create universes from the simplest combination of letters. Her poems were simple but penetrating and relevant to the time she was living in. They embodied her deep understanding of Iranian society and reflected the true social status of the Iranian women.

Farzaneh Farahanguiz loved Forugh's poems so much that she used to recite them at any occasion she found suitable: at school, friends' parties, and family gatherings. She had memorized every published poem by Forugh. She was attached to their simplicity and uniqueness. Her schoolmates made fun of her for her strange taste. No one else at her school was familiar with this contemporary poet. They knew all about Hafez, Saadi, Rumi, and many other classical poets. The school's principal was an old religious man who did not allow contemporary poetry as part of the curriculum.

Later, when she was studying at Tehran University, Farzaneh came to understand the deep meanings of Forugh's poems and tried to spread the word among her friends. Together with those friends, she organized a student activist group to pursue Iranian women's rights through word of mouth, weekly magazines, and public speeches.

She became famous and infamous instantly; she was followed by many women and chased by government agencies and religious groups.

After graduating, she married Saman Honarmand, the brother of one of her friends.

They had fallen in love with each other after meeting at a student gathering. Within a year, they added to their family, a girl named Nazanin.

Zadi remembered now that the name of Farzaneh Farahanguiz had been all over the magazines. A women's rights advocate, Farzaneh had lived in an apartment in one of Tehran's northern neighborhoods. A place of many legends, of parties and gatherings of famous people.

Farzaneh had begun to receive intimidating messages first, and then threats that she and all her family would be killed. She could not stop what she had started.

First, there was an accident. One morning, Saman was taking their daughter to school in his car. On their way, a heavy van hit the car from behind. Not so hard a hit, but hard enough to make Saman stop and get out of his car. The two vehicles involved in the accident pulled over to examine the damage. Several men quickly surrounded Saman's car, bundled Saman and Nazanin into the van, and drove away. The police found no trace of them or the kidnappers. After thirty days, an anonymous call informed Farzaneh that she could find the bodies of her husband and her daughter in a deep well by a hill in Marvdasht, close to Persepolis. They had dropped them alive into the well and topped the well with a heavy rock. Friends and family searched and found the spot. Saman and Nazanin had died holding each other. Their bodies were partially decomposed. The police could not discover who had committed this horrifying crime.

And then Farzaneh disappeared. Her name was all over the media. Some said she was dead, that she'd died in an accident and had been carried away by the river. Others said she was working as a salesgirl in New York. Others said she had married into royalty at the court of Siam. Soon it became a game in the press, guessing where Farzaneh Farahanguiz could be. Such silly stories. People thought they had seen her in the most unlikely of places. Unkind places. It became a running joke almost: Where is Farzaneh Farahanguiz? Can you find Farzaneh Farahanguiz?

After six months in hiding, Farzaneh managed to escape with a smuggler's help, under the name of Farzaneh Soltani. She went to Turkey, then to Italy, France, and England. She took temporary employment, supported by Iranian expatriates. But she could not get a permanent visa until, at last, a friend invited her to dinner. Her friend's husband was from Argentina. That night, he had also invited the Argentinean ambassador, who helped Farzaneh get to Buenos Aires and apply for a permanent visa.

Maryam was sitting quietly on her bed, thinking and talking to herself.

"They smell of flowers when they don't think anyone is around. There is a sweetness they let out, a kind of secret that feels like they are tickling you, but not through their scent exactly. The perfume is only a cover for something much grander.

"It's like kindness. The real kind, when a mind revolves faster than any single thought, seeing in one instant a person or thing that has happened a million times before, seeing it all, and choosing. It's the choosing. That is what it is.

"These things I know.

"Down by the river where the water is muddy like a coin—there is a world.

"I have gone there with my maman, and I know.

"It is like the Capitan, the way he is swimming inside of himself. I can see the pockets in his body, where there are black spaces. Behind these spaces there are strings, and he pulls on them. He pulls on them when he is unhappy, when he wants to show happiness. He pulls on them and is pulled into himself. And I see his pain. I wish I could help him stop this. This pulling and those dark shadows hurt him more than his coughing. That is nothing compared to this pain.

"These things I know.

"The new lady, the one with the sigh and the beautiful hands, is kind. She is different. I don't think I have ever seen or felt someone like her. She knows things but in a different way from me. She made me want to shout and sing—isn't that something? She will make everyone very happy. She just doesn't know it yet. She is kind but sad. I wonder if one can exist without the other.

"Sometimes sadness is just tiredness.

"Sometimes all we need to do is to sleep a little.

"These things I know.

"Sometimes I get angry. Like Maman, who is everything and still falls into herself, forgets. I wish she would know that it doesn't matter.

"And how or what is pain? Why do we feel it? Why does it visit us?

"Sometimes I can see it, and how to make it better. It suspends itself in the air, the deliciousness of it, hanging in the air.

"But I am lucky to see this. And sometimes I am sad that I am.

"I will miss her. I didn't get to say good-bye.

"These things I know."

Chapter Twenty-Four

She swirled once more. And this is how it ends—no color, just solidity, as she turned on her living room floor.

The little walnut under her breast, the lump. She sensed it was waking, surprised at her gumption. It still had some time to manifest itself into whatever it thought it was—where did it want to go, what kind of life did those cells think they would ever have? She wondered. Didn't they know they were only meant for darkness? No sanctity, no sanctity at all.

It was hard for her to say this, even about a cancerous mass spreading its tentacles across her body. *How Jalalladin's words are still with me,* she thought. *How they have guided everything I have done and felt. Until this moment.*

For now I am about to claim my freedom. Now I feel the most pain of all.

Yes, we would like to think that even this cancer has a need, for why else would it feed, but need is not enough. Necessity is not the beginning, it is not a passport to anything. Necessity is only a mirror, and a warped one at that.

Oh, but she was getting dark. She was letting it take over. This she mustn't do. Sheema Bahrami had warned her of such moments, especially if she decided to go it alone. Sheema had promised to keep her secret, had known the importance of it. Of silence.

This was not the way it normally happened. She knew this. But then how did it normally happen? Lying in a dim room, with people she hardly knew or recognized swirling about her? Positioning her between worlds, wanting her to accept words she knew were inconsequential, unnecessary to that moment, to that truth she had known since she was fifteen years old.

A truth she had perhaps always known. A truth eternal.

She had gone in to see Sheema last month, after waking up to that little walnut. "Well, what do you know?" she had said.

"All these years and it comes to this."

It was funny, but of all people, it was the new woman she was thinking of now, as the colors ceased, and a thinness began to introduce itself through her turning body. She thought of the new woman for some unclear reason. She had some vague but pleasant feeling toward Farzaneh, although she had not found out who Farzaneh was, or why she was here.

She had felt a deep sadness within the woman, but had also noticed how she struggled for some worthy cause.

Everyone had their reasons for coming, for being here. In this building she had named after that glorious woman, on a whim, one Paris morning.

Farzaneh reminded her of something, a moment among the cypresses, the reeds, when the wind was blowing. A moment when she had felt contained but free.

In all the cities she had lived, the beautiful places and people she had come to know—there had been such experiences, such lucky moments (the sugared frangipanis tucked under her blouse as she rode that palomino on a Fijian beach)—through all that beauty, she had been guided by what he had told her, but now she could see that she had only been left wanting more. More of something. She had chased this emptiness, this need all her life, not knowing she was chasing it.

How could he have left her there, left her to fight alone? How could he think she could go on, for the rest of her life? How could he not have known that she was only human?

Years later she went back to Behshahr. She walked that same pine-needled path to the riverbed, with its cypresses. She could smell him, that soap on his body. She reached down and pulled on a handful of reeds, feeling a sudden urge to pull them out, but then left them there. She went back looking for Jalalladin, and his mother. The hut was abandoned. There were a few old pots and pans left hanging on the wall. The wind was funneling through the crumbling walls.

"Well, Jalalladin Ansari," said Haji Khanoum. "I'm coming home."

And so it was. *She is gone,* thought Zadi. *Another one of my beloveds.*

The Capitan had been the one to find her, opening her door the next morning when she had not answered. "I don't know what came over me," he said. "I would never have breached what was proper, but something told me I was needed."

He said this as though he did not understand the words, and his hands came up to his face in horror.

She had been lying on her daybed, her arms crossed, a soft, sad smile on her face.

Collapsing on the floor next to her, the Capitan had begun to cry, loud, racking sobs that woke up Zadi.

She had rushed in to find her friend, the one who had given her the ability to say yes again.

No, it was not possible.

There they were, the two of them, mourning though not knowing it, until Maryam came into the room. Slipping her little hand into her mother's, she woke Zadi to what she had to do.

And now here they were, watching Haji Khanoum be lowered into the ground next to someone to whom, the elaborate tombstone said, she had been married.

How can I have known her and yet have known nothing? thought Zadi. She fingered the envelope the landlord had given her before the funeral; it had been addressed to Zadi, and in it were papers signing over the Anna Karenina and its sundry contents.

"You did not know?" asked Niendo. "She was good at keeping secrets," he said, chuckling, pride in his voice.

Along Calle de Florida they proceeded, a long line of them. At the entrance to the Anna Karenina, Zadi waited as the rest walked up the staircase, Maryam between the Sookoots, then the Capitan, dressed in his gabardine suit, and Parastoo carrying a long-stemmed rose.

Farzaneh Soltani and Houshang were at the rear, each carrying lilies.

But the pain. It was unbearable. *Oh, Haji Khanoum, that day. You saw me and you knew. How did you know, how?* The feeling took hold of her again, after they had all left. A clenching coldness. She curled into herself, breathless. Her love, her Haji Khanoum, her mother and friend.

After the crying, Zadi opened the note Niendo had given her.

Only this. Only this, joon-e man. I was so happy to have you and our Maryam in my life. Nothing could have convinced me to go to some half-life of strange things, that comfort that I had become used to. The sadness it brought to me daily. That listlessness I could not shake. Until I saw you two angels in the airport that day. What joy to have been given that chance! To love again! How could one person be so lucky,

I thought. And I had been afraid. Of being greedy in this desire. Did I perhaps stop you from your true path? Were you meant to see that one again, the American you had talked about only once? But you said once is enough. Maybe. Maybe not.

I don't know much. But this I know:

The little one.

Fear not, for nothing is lost. Maybe you feel like you haven't given enough. That you are not a good mother. That the secret—which I know, joonam, the one from the hammam; you told it to me that day as well, although you may not remember. You told me what doorway you were shown that day.

Did I ever tell you of my travels through America? Of all the places outside our beloved land, and outside our little paradise in the Anna Karenina, that is where I would call home. America. But America perhaps a hundred and fifty years back, in the time of the Wild West shows. (I would have made a magnificent horsewoman, don't you think?)

Those frontier mothers, back when everything was so mysterious to them, they knew about releasing their kind into the unknown. They gave their boys—for they were almost always boys, of course—they gave them an awe of the land and the heavens above, which they saw as the physical manifestation of their communion with the new earth they had inherited.

Those frontier children were taught to think like doctors and scientists, to see everything as a marvel. All the glory of nature, the terror before them.

It is no different from what you have given Maryam. You want to equip her with a map, so that she can have this unknown. Because that is what you have done, Zadi-joon. Even if you don't know it. You have braved so many unknowns.

My brave girl. Keep braving those unknowns.

Love from the one who knows you.

—Nikki Khanoum

. . .

They walked hand in hand after leaving the school, making their way down the avenues. The bandage had come off her little one's wrist, and just as Sheema had said, there was only the faintest shadow of a mark.

Haji Khanoum had said that after losing love, there was no real way to find one's place on earth again. That from that day on, one was always scattered.

It was the one thing Haji Khanoum had said that was wrong, thought Zadi.

Because there was a way of finding it.

They came to the plaza. The women she had heard about, the mothers who gathered there every Thursday, were beginning to move around the monument in the center. They were carrying their signs, and photographs of their lost children. Some even carried lines about the war that was still going on.

With all that had happened, Zadi had forgotten about the war.

She and her daughter stood watching the mothers, then walked on to the Anna Karenina.

"Zadi-joon."

Houshang stood in the doorway.

She looked at him. He was dressed in his work suit. His eyes were red.

"It exists."

She stared back at him. She felt like there were stones in her chest, in her stomach.

"It exists because it is perfect. It is perfect because it is the only thing. The only thing of which we can be certain.

"That's what Descartes says. God exists because he is perfect. Do you not see, Zadi-jan? Don't you see what I see?"

She looked at him for a moment longer, breathing in and out slowly.

"Yes."

"Yes?"

She smiled. A space opened up in her chest. She felt it filling and emptying all at the same time.

He took her hand.

They turned and walked inside.

> *This body, O youth, is a guest house,*
> *Every morning a new guest arrives*

They all sat around the carpet once again. Zadi began the poem, stopping after the first quatrain to look around. The Capitan met her eyes and repeated:

> *This body, O youth, is a guest house*

"Haji Khanoum would have liked it."

> *This body, O youth, is a guest house,*
> *Every morning a new guest arrives.*
> *Don't say this guest is a burden to me,*
> *for he may perish into non-existence.*
> *Whatever may come to your heart from beyond,*
> *welcome them as your guests and entertain them.*

Farzaneh Soltani looked at Zadi, and then her hands, which were folded.

She sighed.

She just wanted to be. For a time, a minute. And we will see. We will see.

Whatever may come to your heart from beyond,
welcome them as your guests and entertain them.

Homa looked at Reza.

"The subject tonight is love," Reza yelled. "And tomorrow night as well. As a matter of fact, I know of no better topic for us to discuss until we die!"

She will wait. She will wait, and when the right time comes for her, she will know.

Then she will take those jewels they kept under their mat and throw them into the Rio de la Plata.

She will get rid of them, and she will go.

Until then, she is going to talk of Hafez. And Attar and Rumi. She is going to sing those poems at the meetings. She is going to sing those poems.

This body, O youth, is a guest house.

Parastoo sat thinking.

That was Iran, another place, another world, another time, thought Parastoo. That was the way it was for her then. She did not choose to walk out, because there was never that option. There was never a moment, never a pause. To think beyond the questions.

She remembered what Khanoum Ghavami had said. It is what it is. Khanoum Ghavami was right. It is what it is, but it isn't what it is. But . . .

Every morning a new guest arrives.

Haji Khanoum had encouraged Parastoo to spend the night at Zadi's the night before, telling her she needed some time alone. She had known and chosen.

This body, O youth, is a guest house,
every morning a new guest arrives.
Don't say this guest is a burden to me,
for he may perish into non-existence.
Whatever may come to your heart from beyond,
welcome them as your guests and entertain them.

Zadi was holding Haji Khanoum's letter when Maryam woke up. The girl crawled from her mat and put her arms around Zadi, her head resting on her lap.

Zadi cried, brushing her fingers through Maryam's long hair. Wiping her tears, she said, "There are things I have to tell you, Maryam-joon. Things about your father."

Maryam looked up at her with those big eyes. "Some things you don't need to know, Maman-jan."

Zadi thought of her pregnant body that day in the hammam. How large and foreign she had felt.

Leaning against the bathhouse wall, her hands against the tiles as she strained to hear the melody coming from the other room.

But there are other things you do need to know, Zadi thought, looking at her child. *One day I will tell them to you, my love.*

"Not everything needs to be known, Maman."

Yes, joon-e man. Ghalb-e man.

When destitute and in need, let your love and passion
breed,
Life's alchemy, essence and seed, unimagined wealth
shall create.

They looked up to see the Capitan walking along the corridor. The old man was lost in his own thoughts.
This is life, he thought. *Life is something.*

Something to hold, something to understand.

He had sent word to his daughter. She had left for that river, with the love that was due her. *She will do great things there,* he thought, things they could not even have imagined.

> *When destitute and in need, let your love and passion*
> *breed,*
> *Life's alchemy, essence and seed, unimagined wealth*
> *shall create.*

And so what? And still he did not know.

And still he would go for a walk, watching for the sun, listening for those sounds, those bare feet on the floor, for the love that somehow still bounced around his throat, his heart.

How was this possible? How could his heart still keep beating?

He did not know.

The need to burst into love, the need to keep going forward, most of all to remember, and to forget.

How foolish he may seem to some.

To still want, to need so much.

Afterword

As my daughter, Marsha, wrote in a note in 2009, the idea for this book came to her in 2001 after a confrontational telephone conversation with her mother, which triggered recollections of her childhood memories. She turned to her computer and began to type. Not verbatim, not word for word what had transpired, but a hasty memo. Due to her involvement in other projects, however, including writing her first novel, *Pomegranate Soup*, Marsha had to postpone the act of writing for a later date—leaving the idea at the periphery.

In 2008, after she had published her first two books, she turned her attention back to that original idea. She did not know then that she was embarking upon a daunting task, one that would keep her occupied for the following six years. As she put it later, when the idea first reared its mutant head, it was not so much a book as an elusive mental image of a scene—a meshing of childhood memories and imagination.

Marsha was less than two years old when her mother and I were accepted to the University of New Mexico to continue our postgraduate degrees in America. We packed and were ready to go and were waiting for our visas from the US embassy in Tehran. Less than a day before it would have been our turn, we heard that the embassy was besieged and its personnel held hostage by the revolutionary students. Our dreams of studying in America perished.

However, we decided not to give up. We decided to go to Argentina with the hope of getting a visa from the US embassy there. It would take more than four years, but we would finally get our visas.

In Buenos Aires, while we waited, we managed to rent the fifth floor of a large building, much of which was sublet to other Iranian families. In this house, Marsha experienced the distinctive culture of the Iranian diaspora. Her memories of this time were the foundations upon which she built the narrative of this book.

Soon after we arrived in Argentina, Marsha's mother, who had learned the art of facial-hair removal using band andazi, or threading, secured a few clients. Gradually, our house became a gathering place for Iranian expatriates, especially women. It was a place to get information, to hear and tell stories, to exchange gossip, and to find new friends.

When Marsha was seven, we moved to Miami, Florida, where again Marsha expanded her cultural knowledge while gathering and storing essential ingredients for her future stories. With us, she participated in Iranian gatherings, including poetry nights enriched with live music. Marsha, who was learning to play the piano, got the chance to show off by playing some elementary songs; she enjoyed the attention and admiration.

At school in Miami, Marsha was identified as gifted and was selected for a special educational program designed for exceptional children. Marsha loved both music and books. She studied piano for eight years, including a year at the Elder Conservatorium of Music in Adelaide, Australia. However, her love for books and writing surpassed even her fanatical desire to master the piano and to become a concert pianist.

While her childhood memories provided the initial inspiration for this book, the act of writing gradually became a means to explore her favorite subjects: beauty, love, and metaphysical truth. She challenged religious beliefs, engaged in mystic practices, delved into Sufi's illusive doctrines and rituals. Searching into the past, recollecting, interpreting, and reflecting upon her memories became both a way to gather material and a medium for exploring and remaking her views of the world and her place in it. To this end, Persian poetry provided her with vital insights.

In Persian culture, which had deeply penetrated Marsha's psyche, there is a strong tradition of communal recitation and interpretation—of reading poetry together, and together reflecting upon its meaning. This tradition attracted her attention as a precious cultural phenomenon. She embellishes the pages of this book with some profoundly meaningful poems and challenges readers with ambiguous and controversial verse. This was a formidable task and demanded research and study. It was even more daunting for someone who had not lived in Iran long enough to learn the language and had not been fully immersed in the culture of her birthplace—a culture that cannot be faithfully expressed in translation.

She rushed to Persian literature and found an ocean of love, beauty, meaning, and mystery. She was determined to extract the essence from that ocean and to mix it with her own childhood memories in order to make this book her best and her most profoundly meaningful. Her commitment to this monumental undertaking preoccupied her and became a major cause of her lack of attention to her mental and physical health.

In that 2009 note, she wrote: "I've spent the last five months working on the edit for my third book. It has been a painful process, to say the least. Hardly a night has passed that I have not woken up midway through sleep, body drenched in sweat, heart beating out the rhythms of some ancient tarantella inside my chest. My legs throbbed, both during the day and at night—the kind of throbbing that shook whatever seat I was on—and I looked like I had aged ten years, eyes drooping, skin ashen, a vague recollection that I had not washed my hair for a week straight." As far as I am aware, these conditions persisted for more than five years, ending with her death in April 2014. Marsha had completed the manuscript in 2008 and 2009, setting the story in Los Angeles. Then she rewrote it, setting the scene in Buenos Aires. There are so many versions of the book, which demonstrates her continuous effort to achieve perfection and to leave a precious legacy for generations to come.

I was aware of Marsha's engagement in writing this book right from the beginning. Occasionally, she asked me questions when she needed information or clarification. However, my real involvement with the book began when Marsha came to stay with us for six months in 2012. During this time, we discussed the book, its title, and the main ideas behind it. Marsha used to read her text out loud, and I was to listen carefully and criticize it, although she did not like criticism, especially from her father. Then she gave me a copy of the manuscript to read (and invited me to offer suggestions, if I dared). At the same time, she was contacting publishers and agents. In June 2012, she went to the United States to finish the book and hopefully to sign a contract.

After Marsha's death, I learned that her delivery of the final manuscript was long overdue and that the last version, sent to HarperCollins Australia, was far from being complete. I realized that her book might not be published at all. I had lost my precious daughter, and I didn't want her six years of intensive work to perish forever. I knew Marsha's desire to give this book to the world, and I became determined to deliver it for her. I set out to review the many versions and her hundreds of scattered notes. I checked the English translations of the poems to ensure they were true to the meaning of the original Farsi.

In undertaking this task, I experienced many mixed emotions. I repeatedly found myself crying, either as a proud or as a mourning father—sometimes as both.

This book can be described as a contemporary allegorical narrative, similar to *The Conference of the Birds*, which was written in verse by the Persian poet Attar in the twelfth century. In Attar's poem, the birds of different kinds decide to find their legendary leader, Simorgh. They all set out to pass through seven harsh and difficult valleys of spirituality and enlightenment. Many of them cannot overcome the hardship and die or abandon their search. Only thirty birds reach their destination on the top of Mount Qaf, where they believe Simorgh resides. However, they cannot find their imaginary master. The birds look at each other and realize that they themselves are Simorgh. In the Farsi language, the word *si* means thirty, and the word *morgh* means birds; therefore, Simorgh was nothing but the thirty birds who reached their destination; they are God, and God is them.

In Marsha's book, a group of Iranians of diverse backgrounds come together. Like the birds, they find that in concert, they can search for divine inspiration within themselves. Blessed with an abundance of cultural and spiritual guidance, and equipped with their ancient art of storytelling, they set out on their life journeys, buoyed by unity and togetherness.

Thanks to my wife, Debbie, and my son, Darius, for their patience and support during this hard time.

—Abbas Mehran, October 2014

A Glossary of
Words and Phrases

Persia or Iran, Persian or Iranian?

You might have wondered why the terms *Persian* and *Iranian*, and *Persia* and *Iran*, have been used interchangeably in this book. There are many non-Iranians who think that the name of Iran was formerly Persia, and that the Pahlavi Monarchy changed it to Iran in the twentieth century.

This is a misunderstanding. Iran has always been called Iran in the Iranian native language; however, in the Western world, the name Persia was commonly used. In 1935, the Iranian government asked foreign delegates not to refer to Iran as Persia. Later, in 1959, it was decided that both names could be used interchangeably. So "I am Iranian" is the same as "I am Persian." In Iran, however, I am always Iranian.

Agha. Sir.

aghd. Marriage ceremony, religious or legal.

Ahriman. Evil.

Ameh. Paternal aunt.

Ashura. The tenth day of the month of Muharram. Shia Muslims regard this as a day of mourning for the martyrdom of Hussein, son of Ali, the grandson of the Prophet Muhammad, killed by Yazid in the Battle of Karbala.

atr. Perfume.

Avesta. The holy book of the prophet Zoroaster, the founder of the Zoroastrian religion, which originated in Iran around 600 BCE.

Avicenna. Also known as Ibn Sina, was born in AD 980, and was one of the most famous Persian mathematicians, philosophers, and astronomers.

azizam. My dear.

baba. Father, dad.

Baba Taher. An eleventh-century mystic Persian poet.

barbari. A type of bread, similar to Turkish bread.

bazaar. A covered marketplace.

birun. What is visible on the outside, what is apparent.

chador. A large piece of cloth used to cover a woman's body from head to toe, except for the face.

Dariush Bozorg. Darius the Great, the Persian emperor who built the palace of Persepolis.

darun. What is inside, what is not apparent.

deevoon-e or divooneh. Mad, crazy.

divan. A complete volume of a poet's verse; also, a wooden bank.

dugh. A drink made of yogurt, water, salt, and other spices or flavorings.

ehsaas. Feelings.

eshgh. Love.

fani. Mortal.

Farsi or *Parsi.* The language primarily spoken in Iran.

garm. Warm.

gaz. An Iranian confectionery, known in English as nougat.

ghalb. Heart.

ghalyun. Water pipe.

ghazal. A type of poem consisting of rhyming couplets and a refrain; each line shares the same meter.

gheimeh. An Iranian casserole made with meat, potatoes, split peas, and preserved lemon.

Ghiyamat. Judgment Day.

gholaam. Slave.

ghondagh. A piece of cloth and a rope used to swaddle infants.

golestan. A flower garden, and the title of one of the poet Saadi's books.

Haji. Someone who has made a pilgrimage to Mecca to pay respect to the Prophet Muhammad, pray, and participate in religious ceremonies.

Haji Firooz. A wandering musician who announces the coming spring and the New Year by dressing in red, painting his face black, dancing, and playing the tambourine.

Haji Khanoum. A female Haji, that is, a woman who has been to Mecca.

hammam. Public bathhouse.

heech. Nothing, zero.

ihram. A sacred state that Muslims must enter before completing a pilgrimage to Mecca.

Inshallah. If God wants.

jan. Dear, a term of endearment, used alone or appended to a person's given name.

jennie. Also known as a jinnie or a genie, a supernatural creature.

joon. Dear.

joonam. My dear.

joon-e man. My dear.

Kaaba. A cuboid building in the center of the Mosque of Al-Masjid al-Haram, in Mecca, Saudi Arabia; all Muslims should pray facing Kaaba.

Khanoum. Lady, madam.

Khoda. God.

kolliyat. An author's oeuvre or body of work.

Koran. The holy book of Islam.

Leili va Majnoon. Layla and Majnun, two characters in a love story by the Persian poet Nizami Ganjavi.

lezzat. Enjoyment, gratification.

Madres de la Plaza del Mayo. Mothers of the May Square—mothers of the lost children of Argentina.

maman. Mother, mom.

mast. Drunk.

mateh. An herbal tea common in Argentina.

Mullah. A Muslim clergyman.

na. No.

nafs. Conscience.

Nourooz. New Year's Day.

pari. Fairy.

Peer-e Sabz. The Green Man, one of the ancient prophets.

Qajars. The Qajar dynasty, which ruled Iran between 1785 and 1925.

rusari. A headscarf.

Safavians. The Safavids dynasty, which ruled Iran from 1501 to 1722.

Sahra. An outdoor picnic area.

sefidabeh. A white powder used for cleaning the body and face.

Shahnameh. The Book of Kings, written by the poet Ferdowsi.

Shaitan. Satan.

sharm. Shame.

sofreh. A large piece of cloth on which food is served.

sohbat. A chat.

taarof. The custom of refusing to accept a favor or a gift, even though you may really want it, as a sign of pride and good manners; also, offering to give when you really can't or don't want to.

tawhid. Unity, the doctrine that there is only one God.

ta'ziyeh. A religious theater.

tomans. Iranian money.

tombak. A type of drum.

toot. Mulberry.

torshi. Pickled vegetables.

Tudeh. A communist party in Iran.

Ya-Haqh. Oh God, God is truth.

Zekr. The names of God, the act of reciting them.

About the Author

Photo © Jordan Matter

Marsha Mehran was an international bestselling novelist with a multinational identity. She was born on November 11, 1977, in Tehran, Iran, and she lived in Iran, Argentina, America, Australia, and Ireland. Her first novel, *Pomegranate Soup*, was published in 2005 and became an international bestseller. The sequel, *Rosewater and Soda Bread*, was published in 2007. This novel, released in Australia in 2014 under the title *The Margaret Thatcher School of Beauty*, has also been translated into Italian and Polish. She died in Ireland in April 2014.